Albatross Crossfire

The Crossfire Team acquires a new member with a mission which is critical to their continued existence. The Team learns of a new enemy that is the largest and most connected and funded they've ever encountered beyond the RHONE. They give up their Sea Base to protect Israel and Tel Aviv's inhabitants from attacks on themselves and become a moving target.

- Stephen L. Thompson

Albatross Crossfire

Published by
Stephen L. Thompson
Facebook.com/CrossfireNovelSeries

Unless otherwise noted, Scripture quotations are taken
from the HOLY BIBLE, NEW INTERNATIONAL VERSION®.
Copyright© 1973, 1978, 1984 by International Bible
Society. Used by permission of Zondervan Publishing
House. All rights reserved.

ISBN- 978-1-943879-25-0

Published in the United States of America

Albatross Crossfire

Albatross Crossfire

"New Levels, New Devils"

Stephen L. Thompson

Foreword

To my Christian readers –
The Crossfire continuing series of action-adventure novels include depictions of violence which are unusual in Christian literature. It would be nice if there were no conflict or violence in our world. But we live in a time when evil is increasing instead of diminishing, when some men seem to be controlled by selfishness, madness, or evil forces. When the enemies of decent mankind are bent on subjugation of other men and women, righteous men and women must stand against evil. The yoke of oppression is not lifted by prayer alone. God is our shepherd and we are his sheep. As long as there are wolves about, God will use some of us as sheep dogs to defend the rest of us. These stories are about people like that and the forces they fight against. The stories describe violence because it occurs in the real world and it is active in the lives of all people whether they recognize it or not.

To my non-Christian readers –
The Crossfire series include depictions of spiritual warfare and spiritual activity with which the non-Christian reader may not be familiar. These stories describe the realms and activities of both God and Satan because they're real and active in the lives of all people whether they recognize it or not.

Steve Thompson

Foreword

CHAPTER ONE

Ethan Reaper stood totally absorbed, looking into the workout area just below where he stood. He had seen pretty women and even beautiful women before, but he was watching Christi Steele working out and realized that something was drawing him to her. He also realized that he wasn't breathing. She was a beautiful blonde-haired young woman with curves and determination. She was 5 foot, 6 inches and as he saw it, she was perfect in all dimensions.

Seeing motes floating in his eyes, Ethan gasped in some air and promptly forgot about breathing again. Ethan was 5 feet, 10 inches in height and weighed roughly 178 pounds. He was trimly athletic and not bulked out; but, of course, his tattoos turned some women on and drove others away but, he had them and they weren't going away.

His blue eyes were intense, and he was talented enough to have been chosen to be the head of the COMM/SEC group. He was also quickly becoming an accomplished warrior under the same training that the object of his fascination was going through at present.

He had said, "Hi" to her a week ago and she returned his greeting. But, that was it. She was driven by a mission from Yahveh God and nothing else had a chance to interfere with that. He sighed and headed up to his department and another day of excitement. As he moved along he realized what it was that had him so attracted. It was her spirit. His spirit recognized her spirit as a kindred spirit. He would have to think and pray on that.

Back in the workout area, Christi was attempting to complete all her reps in less time than the last round. She had always worked hard at everything she did. After getting used to the eight different trainings she was going through at the Crossfire Team's Sea Base, she had acclimated to the routine and was extremely focused. Still, she had noticed the head of COMM/SEC staring at her from the window on the second floor rest area. She had promptly forgotten that rabbit trail as she shaved eight seconds off of her record so far. She tackled the next machine.

Two weeks later Christi walked into the War Room and sat down next to Jack. "Hi. I think my head will probably explode soon from all the training being crammed into my mind."

Jack sat back and grinned at her. "I'm keeping track of your progress in your classes, exercises, and tests. Everyone is rating you highly and you're doing very well on all fronts. Of course that is a given because Yahveh would not have put you in this position unless he was sure you would succeed in everything you do. Remember? There is no such thing as coincidence?"

Christi nodded her head. "Yes, and I know I will get through all the classes. I just wanted to ask you if there is any way I could get a phone call to Rachel without compromising either us or her."

Jack nodded, "I'll get a secure link through the Mossad agents in the U.S. Just be careful not to give Rachel too much information that might cause a possible listening party to want to pry it out of her, okay?"

Christi nodded again. Jack called Ethan and had him set up the call. Christi went to the War Room desk assigned to her and tapped in Rachel's number for the call.

Rachel and Christi had suffered through their teenage years together as they completed high school as best friends and confidents. They had supported each other as one or the other met the "perfect "guy" and eventually fell out of love and "got over" the relationships, several times for each of them. Then they each went to a different local college but maintained their friendship through it all. Rachel evolved into a slim beauty with good acting skills and a photogenic élan that made her "desirable" for acting jobs. Her dark hair and intense brown eyes hid a generous heart and a spirit committed to Jesus, her Savior.

Christi knew the time difference in Denver was nine hours behind Tel Aviv time. That would make it around 7:00 A.M. in Denver.

Rachel answered the phone a little groggy, obviously having been awakened by the phone. "Hello?"

Christi said, "Hey, how's the next Oscar winner today?
"Christi!"

Christi laughed, "Yeah, it's me. I don't have much time to talk so I just called to tell you that I am okay."

Rachel laughed too. "How are you doing, working out the complications to your goldenness?"

Christi sighed, "It looks to be a major project. I have no idea how long I will be here.

Rachel thought about that. "I'm really wrapped up in my acting. I've still got a couple of more months on this new film. Send me some pictures of Israel."

Christi saw Su Li waving at her from the door of the War Room. "Opps, gotta go. Bye."

She hung up and smiled at Jack in thanks. She then ran out of the War Room to catch up with her Martial Arts teacher in time for her Jui Jitsu class.

Two hours later Christi had paged Jack to ask to see him for a few minutes after her classes; she walked into the War Room again. She found Jack and Mark Connelly talking. She took a seat and quietly evaluated Mark while she waited.

Mark was a very desirable man. He was in his early thirties. He looked a bit like the character that was portrayed as "Superman" to her. He was over six-foot-tall and had a bulked out physique with large arms, strong legs, a large chest, and flat abs. He looked like someone who could easily represent any of the NFL football teams or possibly the U.S. Marine Corp.

Mark had an honorable face that was also on a Hollywood Star level with well styled dark black hair and an easy grin. He was probably a bit of a cutup too. The vibrations in the spirit that she got were that he was definitely a "White Knight" personality and a protector of anyone who couldn't take care of themselves. Mark was decidedly a good man to know if you had trouble.

While she liked him for his obvious abilities and his good looks she had no interest in him. It wasn't that she couldn't have enjoyed his company, but she also knew and respected the assassin he was married to, Sarah. She was definitely a good woman to know and one not to irritate by being anything except a good friend and fellow warrior to Mark.

Anyway, after talking with Sarah, Christi could tell she was definitely in love with Mark and it was obvious that Mark felt the same way about Sarah.

When Christi caught Mark staring at her while she was staring at him, she jumped up and went over to the two men.

She sat down with a questioning look on her face. Jack asked, "What can we do for you?"

Christi asked, "I appreciate that I'm getting valuable training in all the fields the Crossfire Team deals with. I also know that we are either prepared for or preparing for more battles with the demons of Satan and the human tools Satan uses. My question is this; will I be going with the Team when there is conflict?"

Jack and Mark looked at each other. Jack nodded his head and gestured with his right hand from Mark to Christi. Mark turned to Christi, "I have been evaluating your progress in your classes and while you lack any experience in actual battle, with the one exception, you have shown a good talent and are meeting your marks in everything. The reason I am evaluating you instead of Jack is because Jack excused himself of that role due to his relationship with you. We don't want any envy or anger due to that relationship. Are you all right with me being the leader that is evaluating you?"

After Christi nodded her approval, Mark said, "The answer to your question is, yes. I want you with us so that we can continue to train you "Hands On" during battle, and somewhat protect you until you become completely battle certified. That way you will also have every chance to fulfill your mission, whatever that is."

Christi smiled, "I am pretty sure that we won't know what my mission is until it's time. I haven't gotten a word, a hint, or a clue as to what that mission is as yet. This is regardless of the amount of prayer I am involved in."

CHAPTER TWO

An indeterminate distance from where Christi sat, Carol Moffet was floating over the Matrix of events and interpreting the future events for the Crossfire Team.

She also had been a young, single woman who had visited the Crossfire Team when asked to advise them about her specialty. During her visit, the Team had responded to a demonic problem in downtown Denver. It turned out to be a trap. Jack and Laura had been kidnapped by a demon bent on revenge. After the Malone's had been broken out of the closet of the demonic realm by an Angel, God had healed them of their wounds. Then, to be able to explain why He had let that happen, The Father took everyone involved to Heaven in the spirit.

Given a mind that could understand the interaction of eleven dimensions and also given supernatural knowledge, they had been shown many things including the Matrix in explanation of the event that happened at that time. God had returned everyone and selected Carol to be the Heavenly interface of the Matrix for the Team. Whenever God requested her to read the Matrix or events required her to interpret the Matrix, she would go into prayer and visit the Matrix in her spirit.

The Matrix was like an immense time line floating in some dimension that included all requests of God and approvals or denials. Everything Satan wanted to do to the Crossfire Team and when he requested permission it was posted on the Matrix. Of course there were millions of ongoing and future things moving through time on the Matrix. Carol had literally had over six years of training in Heaven by the Angel Hugo on how to read and interpret the Matrix. She could only deal with things that involved the Crossfire Team. But, in itself that was a full workload.

The Father had also given Carol a set of symbols to show that she was interacting with the Matrix. A white diamond at her throat and another one on her forehead would shine with the Esteem of Yahveh like the swords that went with the armor. These two symbols indicated that her mind and her voice were the duty that God had anointed her to do.

This time she was very worried when she saw the requisitions that Satan had made before God to move demons into the human dimension so that they could attack the Team. She studied all of the information about the event and then her spirit dropped out of supernatural space and back to the Underwater Sea Base.

At the base, the white diamonds on her forehead and her throat faded out and she thanked the Lord for allowing her to do her job. She then left her apartment and ran down the stairs to the War Room.

As Carol entered the War Room she saw Mark and Jack and she went over to them. Jack looked up as Mark continued working with the new member of the Team, Christi Steele.

Carol explained the Matrix sighting and her interpretation of the event. "I'm concerned about this one Jack. They have gotten permission to attack the Team but there are indications that they are going to do it a new way that isn't revealed on the Matrix."

Jack asked, "How many demons, where, when, and why?"

Carol nodded her head. "There are thirty-five demons; they are going to appear in the street just outside of the main Portal entrance above the Sea Base, in about an hour, to attack the Crossfire Team."

Jack nodded in response. "Thanks Carol, why don't you get your .50 caliber sniper rifle and join the party?"

Carol smiled and took off to get ready for the battle.

Mark had listened to Carol's conversation while he was working with Christi. He looked at Christi. "Okay, you wanted to come along, here is your first chance. I am going to give you one of the new sets of Body Armor with the Force Generator built in. The rest of us will start the conflict and then I'll tell you when to join us. I want you to have the Generator on all the time. If your mission is critical to the Team's survival, then the demons will know that and focus on eliminating you. I know that they can't do that while the Force Generator is on, but apparently there is something new they are going to try and until I know what it is I want you to hang back until you have more combat experience."

They went to the Armory and tried the new armor on Christi making sure that it fit and worked correctly. Mark sent Christi to the SOG soldier manning the Armory to get the rest of her equipment. He then took out a set of Generators on belts and tried them one at a time. They worked too. He sealed the vault where they were kept and headed back up to the War Room.

Jack had everyone involved the battle meet outside of the Portal ten minutes before the demons were to arrive.

CHAPTER THREE

Christi felt nervous about the upcoming battle. It was one thing to take on a single demon who is about to kill you, a life and death situation that you had thrust upon you and no options. It was something entirely different to take on a huge bunch of demons deliberately.

She finished putting on her combat gear and checked out how she looked in the full length mirror in the Armory. A mirror in the Armory that she was sure was a woman's idea. She squeezed the switch on her body armor to activate the Force Generator. She was rewarded with a green LED and a tingly feeling over her body.

She liked how the Military look made her look tough. Now, all she had to do was be as tough as she looked. The colors were drab, but functional and not there for style. She waved to the SOG veteran who had worked with her. She then ran to the main entry to the Crossfire Base and surprised herself by not being late and not being the last one there.

There were twenty-eight people there and were carried to the elevators in two shuttles. They rode both elevators up, fourteen warriors in each one.

In less than five minutes they were assembled into four seven-person squads on the street outside of the Portal entrance building. The street became deserted as soon as the soldiers came out and formed up.

Mark called her to the side. "Hang out here until I signal you." He pointed at a recessed part of a pillar near the street in front of the Portal. Mark then positioned Carol with her sniper rifle on top of another pillar just to the right of where Christi was.

Mark spread out the other warriors with the missile soldiers to the left side of where the expected attack would occur.

Christi heard a horrible screeching, cracking, and snapping noise and a twenty-foot-tall rift opened between the demonic dimension and the human dimension. Dozens of demons ran, slithered, leaped, hopped and crawled out of the rift as twenty anti-tank missiles went into the rift.

There were dozens of explosions in the demonic realm and debris and parts of ex-living things flew out of the decimated area.

Christi's mind was immediately attacked by feelings of unworthiness, total failure, a desire to kill herself and die and be done with everything. She suddenly had major feelings of ugliness, sliminess, and illness. Her skin felt like it was crawling with detestable things. It was a heavy attack on her spirit and body. She hadn't expected these demonic attacks and nobody had warned her about them, wait, Laura did mention it in her Spiritual Warfare class.

Alexis, a seasoned member of the Team stepped over to Christi and laid her left hand on Christi's right shoulder. The anointing Alexis carried made the curses and feelings drop away like filthy rags. Christi's normal personality surged back and brightened her hopes and her faith. Alexis whispered in her ear, "Christi, proclaim who you are in Christ and use your spiritual armor to defeat the enemy's curses and lies. Alexis then left and ran back toward the enemy.

Although this was her first physically spiritual battle with the team it didn't seem as if the Team was faring too well. Somehow the Team's warriors were locked into place and the slimy demons freely attacked all of the warriors. The Team was protected by the Force Generators but couldn't move well enough to strike the demons to terminate them.

Jack keyed the "All Members" call switch and talked to everyone. "This is something new. They can move and we can't, but, they are stymied by the Force Generators and can't physically get at us. They do have a device that generates a spiritual harmonic or frequency that affects the Force Generator field and that humming is beginning to affect some of our troops. It seems to seep into our souls and is trying to affect us one at a time. I've prayed against them with no results so I think we're being blocked in the spiritual so that we can't call on Yahveh, Yahshua, or the Angels. This is beginning to wear us down. They may have found something to counter our best efforts. Keep the faith and fight when you can with whatever works."

Christi was shocked. This was the first time she had heard that the demons could out-do the Crossfire Team.

Instead of fear and worry she found herself full of anger at the demons and determination to save the team.

She thought of all the ways she had been trained to defeat demons and selected on the only one she could see that would work. She prayed to the Father for approval to do what she had planned. She didn't feel any disapproval and her armor and sword flashed into existence. She stepped out of the recess in the pillar that had prevented the demons from seeing her and "saw" in her mind, the demons being removed out of her way.

As Christi truly "saw" the demons being removed and freeing up her path in front of her, she was awed by the destructive power of the Force Generator that she had released. In a blink of an eye the demons disintegrated. Glass exploded from every window in all the buildings in front of her as well as all the vehicle's glass as far as she could see. The demonic rift fractured and dissolved and was gone. She noticed that all the pavement, curbs, and grass exploded away from her. Cars and trucks exploded into fragments. One of the demons on top of Ethan's Force Generator field bubble disintegrated into tiny bits which blew away like in a windstorm.

The Team members were completely protected and rooted where they were in their Force Generator fields. After the blast, they were still where they had been before it.

Freed from whatever the demons had done, Jack walked over to Mark. "Who did that?"

Mark looked around, "From the direction of the blast and the scattering of the debris field, I would say that Christi did it."

Christi walked up to the two men. "I just hope I didn't kill or wound any innocent civilians."

Jack put his arm around Christi's shoulders. "I'm just glad you did whatever you did. They almost had us there. What did you do?"

Christi looked up at the much taller man, "I just used the Number 2 option that Sarah told me about on how to move with the Force Generator."

Jack nodded his head. "I had forgotten that one."

Mark said, "I remembered it, but I held off because I wasn't sure it would be wise use it due to its extreme power and destructiveness."

CHAPTER FOUR

After the Team returned to the Sea Base, finished their After-Action reports, cleaned up, they had something to eat. The Core Team got together to discuss the event. This was something new to Christi, but she realized she was truly welcomed into the Team as a full member now.

Not having any clue what the demons did, or how they did it, Jack asked for Raquel's participation.

Christi was familiar with seeing the Angels Rose and Caleb, but the Archangel Raquel was new and impressive to her.

Jack told Raquel about their inability to move while the demons could move. He also told the Archangel about the spiritual penetration of the Force Generators by the demons.

Raquel thought for a while and then asked Jack to wait. He disappeared for about eight minutes. When he returned he smiled. "Between you and Mark, I can honestly say that I've never, ever, seen anyone that drives Satan as crazy as you two do. God may well have to destroy Satan by His own hand and rewrite all human history; including Bible prophesy.

Mark smiled back, "I'll bet that is a line item for a resume that no one else has ever had. Did the Most High tell you how the demons were able to do what they did?"

"That is precisely why Satan is in so much trouble with the Most High. Satan used several old tricks he had previously sworn to God he would never use again. He defied God again and used things from the eleventh dimension which God forbade him to use ever again".

"I'm not sure I can tell you how they did what they did but, possibly I can explain some of the main features. To accomplish your immobility, Satan, who time does not affect, had demons go to that location and play out all of the steps at several different times, like several hundred different times. Then, when you appeared, they enacted the play at a time when you weren't there. To you, it seemed like they could move and attack you while they weren't doing it, rather, they did it before when you couldn't move because you weren't there that time."

Raquel looked embarrassed, "I am sorry but that is the only way I can understand it. You and those demons never met. How Christi "blew them away" with the feature of the Force Generator is easier. The power in that blast, applied to the demonic forces, destroyed every one of the hundreds of times they had done the operation and then blew away the dimensional rift which coalesced all the versions of the demons into one exceedingly horrendous explosion deep within the demonic realm. The penetration of the Force Generators by their spiritual force was again a function of the time differences applied to your spirits, wherever they were, at the times they made their repetitions. The multiple attacks had to hit some of your members when they were sensitive to the frequency of demonic spiritual attacks."

Raquel could tell that his human friends didn't comprehend what he was trying to tell them. He sighed and shook his head. "Let me explain it this way. Satan violated dozens of different rules and restrictions in an effort to destroy you. They used multiple attacks, when you weren't there, and, which were illegal because they had never asked permission from the Most High to enter your dimension. That is also why the separate attacks never appeared on the Matrix. When they were ready, they posted one attack on the Matrix, knowing that you would respond. They then played like a physical video of the attack. Your bodily beings couldn't move because you weren't really in the same time dimension as the attackers. They could move because it had already been done. If your video recorders could see them it would show you that they stabbed where there was no one, jumped when there was no reason to do it."

"They did a lot of things out of sync with you because you and they weren't there at the same time. Anyway, I can't even tell you how much the Most High is constraining demons because of this. You truly are making Satan so frustrated he is in danger of being eliminated by the Most High. Again, what they did cannot be done again." Raquel noticed that his last attempt to give them understanding was successful.

Jack nodded and Raquel faded away. Jack turned to the others and said, "Well, I guess that sums up the last action. You are all excused except for Christi and Sarah who I need to talk to."

After everyone else had left, Jack turned to the two women. "Christi, I'm sorry to have to tell you this but, in the U.S. you have now become a wanted "person of interest" by the FBI. They are doing everything they can to find you and arrest you. They have no way to know where you are but they will probably bring pressure on your friends, especially Rachel. If you return to the U.S. Marco Marino's henchmen in the FBI will have you detained and questioned. According to our sources, and they are good sources inside the FBI, you will probably be arrested under terroristic warrants and those have no end time due to the Patriot Act."

He looked at the young woman who was presently doing what Yahveh wanted her to do regardless of the costs to her personally. He knew this would be a blow to her and he wanted to tell her before she found out from Denver.

Christi took the news without noticeable anger or discomfort. She nodded her head, "What other costs to me are there in this?"

Sarah put her hand over Christi's to comfort her. "I am very concerned that if they find out you are here they will try to have you extradited as an America Citizen involved in terror activities like they wanted to do to everyone in the Team except David and I because we were Israeli Citizens and they had no rights to demand extradition for the two of us."

Christi sighed, then smiled slightly as she looked at Jack, "And how did you and the rest of the American team dodge that bullet?"

Jack looked squarely at her. "We renounced our American Citizenship and became Israeli Citizens."

Christi asked to be given a few minutes to pray and Jack nodded his agreement to that.

Christi walked out of the War Room and wandered over to one of the couches in the Living Room. Settling down onto the cushions of the couch she began to praise and worship Yahshua and Yahveh. She was about to start praying when she felt someone near her. She opened her eyes and saw the Angel Rose floating in front of her.

Christi smiled at the beautiful Angel and said, "Hi Rose, did you come here to help me?"

Rose nodded her head. "Yes, I did Christi. I knew before you left the United States that this time would come and I have some facts you are not aware of and I think you need to know before you decide anything."

Christi broke into tears and said, "That's good, because I am torn several different ways and I need God's direction and comforting."

Rose settled down on the couch next to Christi. She placed her right hand on Christi's hand and Christi felt a deep peace flood her whole being. Rose's words resounded inside of her and echoed slightly.

"Christi, you know that the Most High looked down through time before the world was set on its axis and saw you and knew you would believe and be a child of His. He wrote your name in the Lamb's Book of Life then. When you were about to be born he called your spirit and gave you a mission and a destiny. You grew and accepted His Son as your Savior. As you grew in the spirit for God, His Holy Spirit lives within you and advises you, heals you, and cares for you. You have stepped up to accept your destiny and your mission and He loves you so much for that and you know He will never abandon you or forsake you. He saw the events of your life reaching a critical juncture and you accepted the warning, the training, and the combat against mankind's enemies, although at the time you weren't consciously aware you had made that choice."

Christi nodded her head as she received the memory of her kneeling before the Throne of God when He gave her the choice and she agreed to fight for Him.

The Angel continued, "I wasn't talking lightly when I told you in your dream that you have a critical mission that will save the Crossfire Team. You have shown you have the heart and the bravery to stand against the odds you will face and win through to victory. No one else can do what you have to do. I can tell you that you and I will be fighting together to win this victory."

Christi nodded her head, "I just miss my past and the people I know and love in Denver. I know now that I will not be able to go back there because the government would take all of it away from me. She teared up again as she thought of the things she would never do and who she couldn't be with anymore.

Rose put her arm around Christi's shoulders and pulled her over until her head rested on the Angel's shoulder. She comforted her until she worked through her tears. Then she looked Christi in the eyes.

Christi gasped inside; she could clearly see eternity in the Angel's eyes. The tremendous vistas and the vast potential for her and love like sunlight poured out.

Rose's voice reverberated in her spirit. "You are a treasure in God's eyes and he will not deny you the desires of your heart, remember that."

Rose released the young woman and drifted several feet away. She smiled at Christi and said, "I salute you, woman warrior of God." Rose whirled into a flash of gold and white and faded away.

Christi closed her eyes and prayed her thanks to the Father and to Yahshua for letting Rose minister to her.

She sat back on the couch and thought about how to arrange her life. Then she laughed a deep, hearty laugh. She didn't have to plan anything, God had that in hand.

She got up and walked back to the War Room and fondly realized she belonged here.

CHAPTER FIVE

Christi stopped to fix up her makeup only to realize she wasn't wearing any. She walked into the War Room and found Sarah there. Christi walked up to her, "I've made my decision. I will become an Israeli Citizen so that I can stay and fight with the Team."

Sarah smiled at her, "One thing you will become used to around here is the interconnection between the Team and Heaven. Rose stopped by to tell us you were choosing to be one of us. Jack had a call he had to take and asked me to tell you he loves you and he is very glad you are living for God and choosing to be one of us. Oh, he also said to tell you that you need to be ready to meet the Prime Minister of Israel tomorrow morning at 9:00 A.M."

Christi wasn't surprised that Jack would know about her decision. She nodded to Sarah, and said "Thank you for your help". She turned to go to her apartment when Sarah said, "Christi."

She stopped and looked at the beautiful but deadly Mossad assassin.

Sarah looked down for a second. Then she looked back at Christi. "I just wanted you to know I am also pleased that you decided to join us. I don't think you know it, but Yahshua Himself took Jack and Laura to Heaven in the spirit where He anointed them to be the Priests of this Team. Just between you and me, I am beginning to see a hint of Heaven in Jack and Laura that wasn't there a year ago. It is like they are moving into a place between Earth and Heaven."

Christi though about what she saw in the Angel Rose's eyes. She smiled a confident smile at Sarah. "I know what you mean; I just saw Heaven and eternity in Rose's eyes." Then she left a surprised assassin and went to her room.

The next morning at precisely 9:00 A.M. Jack, Laura, and Christi were ushered into the Prime Minister's office. In the office were the Prime Minister, General Levy, and Rabbi Chanan. After the introductions, Jack asked the Prime Minister if he would authorize Christi as eligible for Israeli

Citizenship. "I have two sponsors here that will bear witness to her combat worthiness in the defense of Israel."

The PM smiled and said, "I have already talked to my two good friends here and submitted her application for Citizenship and waived the two-year Military requirement. I believe that the videos you sent to all three of us are sufficient to qualify her for Citizenship."

As the two men were talking, Christi got a Word from God. She suddenly stood up and turned toward the door to the office.

As the four men and Laura watched her in surprise she started to pray in her prayer language for power and purpose from Yahveh. Her golden armor and the sword of Yahveh flashed into being and she went automatically into the high guard position with both hands on the hilt of her sword which she held above her right shoulder.

The door was kicked into splinters and one of three gross demons stomped into the room with death in its eyes. Christi went at the demon with a sudden burst of Holy Anger propelling her. Behind her both Jack and Laura's armor and swords appeared and they moved to join Christi in defending the other three men in the office.

The first demon swung his black blade at Christi but she stepped out of its reach and then jumped at the demon and cut its sword arm off at the elbow. The demon started leaking red smoke but turned its right side toward Christi and used its fist to knock her backward. The Force Generator sucked all the power out of the punch, leaving Christi untouched. At that point Christi saw the Angel Rose decapitate that demon.

Jack and Laura had stepped behind the first demon that was fighting with Christi and confronted the other two demons. Jack saw that one of them had a thin blade and looked almost human. It was one of the middle level demons. He wanted to take it on but it was too far to his right and the other demon was charging him. He parried two slashes by the second demon and then chopped straight down and cleaved the demon's head and chest.

Laura knew about the faster reactions and equality of the middle-level demons and approached it carefully. It tried a fake slash and then inverted its sword to thrust it into Laura's chest. Laura side stepped the thrust and completed a right to left slash that caught the middle-level demon at the middle of its neck and decapitated it in the one stroke.

Laura stepped back and her armor and sword faded out of sight. Jack pointed at himself and then the office. He pointed at Laura and Christi and out toward the hall where there was a lot of confusion going on.

Jack came back into the PMs Office to find everyone gone. Jack remembered that the PM had a rabbit hole and it had been used. He went out to help Laura and Christi.

He found a standoff. Laura and Christi had their handguns out and pointed at five Mossad security types who had guns pointed at the women. Jack simply took control of the situation. He walked out between the two parties and told all of them to put their weapons away, NOW!

The women complied while the men were more cautious and slower to accept Jack's command. Jack was praying for two reasons. First, he wanted to make sure there weren't any more demons around, and second, he wanted God's backup on this situation.

His armor didn't appear but it was still a tense situation when suddenly, from thirty feet away, a security man thought that Jack was threatening his fellow security officers and having a clear path he fired his Galil rifle at Jack. It was a three round burst.

Jack recorded the fact that a gun had been fired and he looked toward the shooter. He turned to the security officer closest to him. "Have your man stand down!"

The officer stood there with his mouth open, looking at the Angel Rose and her flaming sword and the three flattened bullets on the floor. She had the look of the wrath of God on her face and he wasn't inclined to argue with her or the man standing next to her. He holstered his pistol and told the rest of the men to do the same.

Quiet and order returned to the situation. Jack turned to Rose and thanked her. She looked at Jack and smiled. Then she swirled into fierce white and gold colors and disappeared.

At that point the PM, who was standing there in some shock, took the three Team members back into his office. Rabbi ben Chanan and General Levy were already there.

The Rabbi shook his head and looked at Jack. "You tend to draw those things don't you?"

Jack shrugged his shoulders. "All part of a day's work." He turned to Christi, "Thank you, sister, you have a sensitivity to oncoming demons don't you?"

Christi shook her head, "No, I got a word from Yahveh and acted on it."

Rabbi Chanan nodded, "Yes, she did. I got the same word but didn't know what to do about it. Thank YHVH that you were here to stop them."

Laura shook her head, "It was probably us that drew them."

Jack shook his head, "No, remember it takes at least fifteen minutes to breach our dimension's walls.

The PM was listening to the chatter and he interrupted to say that he, personally, wanted to thank Christi for alerting them and standing against the powers of darkness to defend them."

Christi nodded, "Thank you for that kind word Mr. Prime Minister. But, that's what the Crossfire Team does and there's no extra charge for this battle."

After the laughter died out the PM made a call and told Jack that the officials were waiting down at the induction office to confer Israeli Citizenship on Christi. He looked at Jack, "I wouldn't want to live your life but I will thank G-d for each and every one of you."

An hour later they were finished with the Citizenship office and on their way back to the Sea Base.

CHAPTER SIX

Laura smiled at Christi after they were in the Mossad SUV on the way back to the base. "You, my dear, are a keeper. Your quick reaction and defense is what saved the day for the three men in the office. I'm not sure that those demons were after us or the PM, the Rabbi, or the General."

Christi sat back in her seat and pointed to the glowing green LED at the collar of her body armor. "I wasn't in any danger. Can we pray about that attack and see what the Father says about the purpose for that raid?"

Jack nodded his head, "I think that is a good idea."

Laura bowed her head and started the prayer. "We thank you, living and eternal King and we praise your mighty and holy name. You are the reason for our being and the love of our lives. Father Yahveh, we come humbly with contrite hearts seeking your wisdom and truth." She touched Christi's arm and fell silent.

Christi picked up the prayer. "Abba, we seek the true purpose for that demonic raid on the Prime Minister's office this morning and pray that Your will be done so that we can fulfill Your purposes for our lives." Christi also fell silent and listened for the still, small voice of God.

Laura was about to start singing a hymn to fill the atmosphere around them when a fourth person was sitting in the SUV with them. Jack recognized the Archangel Raquel and immediately leaned forward and told the Mossad driver not to worry about the sudden addition to their party. The driver's eyes were wide and concerned at the same time but he nodded his head. He had heard about these Judeo-Christians and their frequent visitations by Angels. He hadn't believed it until now. This was going to take some serious Torah study to incorporate real Angels into his paradigm.

Raquel reached over and shook Christi's hand. The FG field didn't seem to affect him. "I am glad to meet you Christi Steele. You were the reason for the attack in the Prime Minister's office this morning. I am not sure if you understand your importance in both our world and that of Satan."

All three of the humans sat there and re-evaluated Christi's role in their lives.

Raquel sensed the shift in priorities. "Christi, your life and your mission are so crucial to the existence of the Crossfire Team that the lives of everyone of the Team, both here and around the world, depend on your continued existence. If you are destroyed, then all of the other people of the Team will be destroyed. The Most High has an important plan for the next three years of the Team's time here on Earth. Without you they will not complete their mission."

Raquel changed into his Angelic form and put his right hand over Christi's head and the anointing motes of light fell over her and she breathed out a large sigh. After that, Raquel sat back and studied her. "The devil knows of your part in all of this and is determined to change history by changing your future. I will be your guardian Angel until your mission is completed."

Raquel turned his bright golden eyes on Jack and Laura, "Look for the enemy to use every weapon at his command to prevent Christi from completing her mission. Also, to complete her mission she must be operating as a member of your Team. Do not secure her in an attempt to protect her. I have given her all knowledge of what you refer to as "spiritual warfare". This is so that she can defend herself from their spiritual attacks. The Most High wants your team to move quickly to bring her friend, Rachel Reynolds from America to the Sea Base so that we can defend her. The enemy wants to use her as a ruse to remove Christi. Be aware of the authorities in the U.S. They are about to do the same thing the demons want to do with Miss Reynolds to have some control over your Team through Christi."

Christi asked the Angel, "Can you tell me what my mission is? I really need to know."

Raquel smiled at her. "No, and the reason I can't tell you is that if you know beforehand it would change the decisions you will make and that would lead to defeat and annihilation for all of you, myself, and many others. Do not worry about what it is. When the time is right you will understand and be in the right place to resolve it."

Raquel smiled at her as he faded out of sight.

Christi shook her head. "Great, if I don't do what I have to do and do it correctly, people I love die, Angels die, and possibly many people die." She grinned, "Oh good, no pressure."

The driver brought the SUV to a halt in front of the main entrance to the Undersea Base Portal. As they exited the vehicle, Jack thanked the driver for circling the block so that they could finish their conversation with Raquel. The driver smiled at him and said, in obvious honesty, "That was my pleasure."

As they rode the elevator down to the Sea Base, Jack put his arm around Christi's shoulders. "We will be with you every step of the way."

Christi patted his hand, "Thank you, that means the world to me right now."

Laura added her assurances and then remarked, "We need to go get Rachel immediately. And, as little as I want to recommend it, Christi, you need to go or Rachel may prove uncooperative."

Christi smiled for the first time since the demons attacked. "Knowing that young lady as I do, I would say that would be an understatement."

Jack thought about that as they got on the transportation cart to cross the Sea Base. "We need to make sure we plan this out so we don't have to have another shooting war with the FBI and the U.S. Military."

CHAPTER SEVEN

As the small Extraction Team boarded the "Myth" they knew that what they were going to do could be very easy or very hard depending on how close they were in timing to the other two groups that had their plans on securing Rachel.

The Myth was a product of the Research and Development or R&D group that had left America and moved to the Sea Base in Israel. The Myth was a new generation of aircraft. One of the leaders of the R&D group, Captain Maxwell, had explained about the plane when they had first seen it. "The Myth is so sneaky it cannot be detected by any radar or sensor look up/down that is known today. It can fly farther, faster, and with an almost non-existent audible signature and visual footprint smaller than anything else flying today. There are two miniaturized CRAY computers on-board and the computer power and sensor arrays are more effective than all those on a new Arleigh Burke or Zumwalt class destroyer. If needed, the Myth can carry almost half of the firepower that is on one of those destroyers." The Myth is capable of vertical landing and takeoff; the jet could also reach speeds of Mach 10 and beyond. As I have told you before with the Ghost and Ghost II, wring it out and bring it back in one piece. Good hunting."

The most unusual thing about the plane was that it was an unmanned aerial vehicle or "UAV". The Myth could hold sixteen passengers. It was a newer version of the "Ghost" and "Ghost II" aircraft the team had used before. Only the Myth was smaller and more effective. Mark had originally protected the Ghost by affixing his body armor with the Force Generator built into it, to the body of the aircraft and could use the "invisible" capability of the Force Generator to hide the whole plane.

Jack had Christi call Rachel and find out what she was going to do that day. It was almost casual chatter but it could give them an idea as to when the FBI would move. There was no telling when the demonic would move.

Christi woke Rachel up again. "Hello next Oscar winner, are you able to talk?"

Rachel responded better this time. "Hi Christi, yeah, I am awake this time. I had a strange dream about guns, fighting, demons, and some stress on my part. I hope that was just the pizza I ate last night."

Christi laughed knowing that was probably a warning dream. "Well, maybe the day will go better than that. What are you going to do today?"

Rachel gave her schedule which didn't start for the next two and a half hours. "I guess I'm going to do my laundry first. Then go to work and make movie magic around 2 p.m."

Christi laughed again. "That sounds positively exciting. Well, I gotta go, so take care and I'll talk to you soon."

As she broke the connection the Myth announced that there were seventy-three separate efforts made to locate Christi's position. There were obviously lots of people listening to that conversation.

Mark commented, "It sounds like the FBI has a full-court press around Rachel. I need to change my original concept of what they are doing. I now think they are not going to grab her and keep her as leverage against us. I now believe that they are going to use her as an "in place asset" to capture us."

Jack sighed, "It can't be easy, can it?"

Mark shook his head. "No, and we still have the wild cards, the demons. They could make their move any time they want to. Plus, I'll bet the demons have eyes on the FBI to prevent them from snatching Rachel first."

Christi laughed, "Then for the demonic, that makes us the wild cards."

Mark laughed with her. "A ray of sunshine in a murky business." He stopped to think for a bit. "That gives me an idea. We need to find a way to get the two groups aware of each other and that may keep them too busy to catch us as we rescue Rachel."

Laura added to the conversation. "What I don't understand is why Raquel couldn't simply transfer Rachel from here to the Sea Base. Why do we have to endanger ourselves as well as Rachel when that would be so simple?"

Christi's newly implanted information gave her an answer for Laura. "Because Raquel would have to get the Father's permission and the demonic would be made aware of that and the demons would strike first. We literally are the unknown wild card to the demonic world."

Mark nodded his head. "I think our newest member has the right of it. Good answer, Christi."

Jack put the image of the floor plan of Rachel's apartment up on the vision screen. "Christi, where will Rachel be doing her laundry?"

Christi took the laser pointer from Jack and pointed to the left of the floor plan. "She has to go to the main floor to the building laundry which isn't on this drawing."

Jack changed the view to a floor plan of the entire building.

Christi pointed to the large room on the first floor. "This is where the laundry is but she could still be in her apartment because she doesn't stay in the laundry while it is washing or drying."

Mark studied the layout. "So, the odds are that she will be in her apartment 89 percent of the time, in transit, 4 percent, and in the laundry 7 percent of the time. I think we need to scout out the apartment first."

Being in "special" mode the Myth was invisible to normal sight. It landed in the nearest empty open field that was two blocks away from Rachel's apartment building.

Jack, Laura, Christi, Mark, and David switched their Force Generators to "special" and left the aircraft and walked to Rachel's building. Since they came in from the front door area they could see that Rachel wasn't in the laundry. They walked up to her floor and stopped. There was a man using lock picks on Rachel's apartment door. There were two more men waiting in a line behind the lock picker. They were wearing body armor, had guns, and vests that read "FBI". Mark walked over to the last man in line and used a stun gun on his neck. Jack took out the second guy the same way. The lock picker saw the two men stiffen and go to the floor. He stood up and Christi swung a hard right hand, upward palm heel strike to his chin and knocked the man out before he knew he was hit.

David tied the men's hands with plastic tie cuffs and shut off the little radio that was asking questions of the unconscious lock picker. Christi switched her Force Generator to "normal" and appeared in the hall. She knocked gently on Rachel's door. A few seconds later Rachel opened the door and saw Christi with her finger over her lips. As an actress she knew that sign language and didn't say a word. Rachel backed up to let Christi in. She tried to close the door but it wouldn't budge. Christi pulled Rachel into the apartment and whispered in her ear. "Don't say anything out loud. The FBI has your apartment bugged and they were coming to arrest you. We are going to get you out of here. If you have anything you love and it's small, get it. You won't be coming back here." The door closed by itself.

Rachel looked at her and shook her head. She whispered back. "The only thing here that I want to keep is our friendship, and you're not that small."

Christi poked her in the ribs and strapped a Force Generator around her waist. She flipped the switch and the LED lit up red. Christ used her battle/COM and said, "Guys, we have a problem." Mark appeared suddenly and looked at the red LED. "Yeah, we do have a problem. We need to get her out of here without the van across the street seeing us."

Jack got a call from Ethan in the COMM/SEC group in the Sea Base. "You guys had better move it. They just rolled up a FBI SWAT team and they are unloading out front."

Mark disappeared again and opened the door. Christi also disappeared but grabbed Rachel's hand and led Rachel out the door followed by the rest of the Team.

They moved quickly down the hall and down the furthest stairs from Rachel's apartment. They got to the ground floor and went out the back gate into the next street.

Christi reached over and removed the Force Generator from around Rachel and secured it in her back pack. The three men and three women ran toward the Myth. A shout from behind them demanded that Rachel stop running. Mark and Jack stopped and told the others to get Rachel onto the plane. Mark keyed the communications link to the Myth and told it to take down the drones in the area. There were three crashes and one small explosion. Now the FBI was without eyes in the sky.

Six men of the FBI's SWAT team in full body armor came running after Rachel. Jack and Mark clotheslined the first two men and knocked the second two men to the ground. The last two fired two quick bursts above their partners. The bullets struck both Jack and Mark's Force Generator fields and fell to the ground.

Jack and Mark ran toward the plane while the SWAT team got the four men on the ground up and organized. Mark was fairly sure they also were calling for backup.

Christi was getting Rachel to the aircraft but they still had a block to go.

Jack and Mark saw the backup coming in the form of a helicopter and a truck full of soldiers. Jack said, "We've got to delay these soldiers or Rachel won't make it to the plane.

Mark said, "Okay, switch to "normal" and let's see what mayhem we can cause." Both men suddenly appeared but the focus was still on Rachel. Mark took out his .40 caliber handgun and put four rounds into the right front tire of the truck. The truck swerved to the right, toward the two men. Mark laughed, "I think that got their attention." The speeding truck hit a curb with its left front tire and that caused the front of the truck to bounce into the air.

The flattened right front tire slammed down onto a fire hydrant which sheared the top off of the hydrant. The water shot out of the hydrant hard enough to tip the truck over onto its left side scattering the soldiers in the back.

The serious momentum of the truck made the back end slide in a clockwise arc to the right and it bulldozed over two of the soldiers before it came to rest. One of the soldiers was screaming and the other one was quiet. Mark shook his head and ran over to the truck and around to the side where the two men were pinned under it. Six or seven soldiers also jumped out and ran to the area of the two pinned men.

CHAPTER EIGHT

To Mark it was just like he was back in the SEALS. He yelled at the men to grab a part of the truck and help him lift it off the men pinned underneath it. Jack was right there with Mark and as more men joined them they were able to lift the truck high enough to allow two other soldiers to crawl under and drag the two victims out and away from the truck. Mark knew the next part could be tricky so he told the men to release the truck and back away. He rested the truck on the Force Generator field while they moved. He then jumped backward and let the body of the truck crash back to the ground. He looked around, "Are any of you guy medics?" There were heads shaken from side to side and a bunch of "No's".

Jack checked the first man and he definitely had a broken and crushed leg. He had passed out. The broken bone wasn't a compound fracture because there wasn't any blood and the leg hadn't swollen up like it had an internal hemorrhage. Jack asked if they had a blanket available. One of the men ran to the back of the truck and brought several blankets. Jack told him to fold one up and put it under the man's head as a pillow and cover him up with a second blanket.

Jack moved over to the unconscious man and checked him for injuries. He couldn't find anything obvious so he probably had a concussion and possibly a head injury. He told the soldiers they needed to get a MediVac helicopter or use the one hanging in the air above them to get both men to a hospital quickly.

As Mark and Jack stood up they realized that the SWAT team that had been chasing Rachel was standing behind them with their rifles pointed at them. Mark walked up and asked the SWAT personnel if they had a supervisor. He ignored their demands to surrender. A civilian was walking toward them and Mark shook his head, it was Russ Holly again. Mark thought to himself, "This will be a big waste of time. At least they got Rachel onto the Myth and out of danger."

Russ Holly walked up and smiled. "Well, well, it looks like you overstepped yourself this time. We've got you."

Mark ignored him and asked the soldier. "I distinctly asked for a supervisor, not a clown."

Russ didn't realize he was dueling with a man who had faced Satan down and looked forward for more fun opportunities to do it again. "You can make all the jokes you want to, but I got you."

Mark looked at the man. "Russ, I fight demons, real demons almost every week. You don't "have" me, and if you want me you'll find I'm more than you can handle."

There was a snicker in the group of soldiers and Russ whirled on the group and stared them down. He turned back to see Mark walking off with Jack. "Hey, stop or we'll fire on you."

Mark looked over his shoulder and said, "That didn't work so well last time, did it?"

Russ had all the troops form up and aim at the two men. There were twenty-four soldiers counting the eight SWAT team members and they all aimed at Mark and Jack. Many of the soldiers weren't going to shoot to hit them because they had helped the two trapped men.

Russ radioed the helicopter to cut the two men off.

The chopper dropped to four feet off of the ground, twenty feet in front of Jack and Mark. It had the same pair of miniguns aimed at them that Mark had used years ago to prevent the overrun of an Army Arsenal.

Russ yelled at them, "If you don't stop immediately I will be forced to fire on you."

Jack was about to tell him to shut up when he saw fifteen to twenty demons spilling out of a rift from behind the soldiers. Jack said to Mark, "Come on, we've got to help them." He started to pray as he ran and his armor and sword exploded into sight. The soldiers were firing at the demons without effect. The helicopter was hamstrung because the demons were on the back side of the soldiers and the chopper's guns couldn't engage the demons directly.

Some of the demons were jumping over the soldiers and turning back to attack them from the rear.

Jack and then Mark ran into the melee and started cutting the demons down. One huge demon slammed his sword into Jack. Jack didn't notice anything and drove his sword through the demon and cut to the side. The demon fell to the ground and started dissolving into gray smoke and demon stain.

Mark went into high speed and took out three of the demons on his side of the soldiers. He dropped back into normal speed and saw one demon reach out and grab Russ Holly with one big clawed hand and raise its sword to cut him in half. Russ was in a panic but he raised his handgun and shot the demon until he was out of bullets. The demon ignored the firing. Mark realized that the demon had hesitated in killing Russ so that he could cause more fear in the man, which was working. Mark stepped up behind the demon and beheaded the beast.

The headless demon dropped his sword and Russ as it fell to the ground splashing demon stain all over Russ' shoes and pants legs. Mark stopped praying for a few seconds so that Russ could see who saved his life. Mark put out his hand and helped Russ up. "See, that's what we fight every day. Excuse me, which side are you on?"

Russ stood there with his mouth wide open. Mark started to pray again and his armor and sword returned. Mark ran between two groups of soldiers and attacked some of the six demons still standing. Two minutes later, Jack held the last demon by the throat and then let him go. He disappeared, still alive. There were no more demons and both men stopped praying. The count was seven dead soldiers and two dead FBI agents. Jack looked worried, "I only counted sixteen demons here. Did the others get to the Myth?"

Mark nodded, "Yes they did. They then ran into the Force Generator field on the aircraft and got jumped by Laura, Christi, and David. The five of them didn't last long."

As they were walking away they walked past were Russ Holly was now sitting on the ground by a pool of demon stain. Mark just shook his head. "Maybe he learned something today."

Jack looked at the frightened man. "He'll probably tell his superiors that we killed all these men. It doesn't matter, does it?"

They reached the Myth. The invisible door opened and the invisible stairs came out. At this point Mark was working in Braille, feeling his way along. Jack had a hand on Mark's shoulder and was right behind him as they entered the plane. The stairs retracted and the door closed. Mark and Jack switched their Force Generators to "normal" and were visible. Mark told the Myth to lift off and get altitude.

The Myth lifted off fifty feet and held there. Two U.S. Air Force F-22 Raptors flashed by a few hundred feet above them. The Myth suddenly accelerated and dropped into a tail chase position behind the Raptors. When they were two miles from Rachel's apartment building the Myth slowed down until the Raptors were a mile away from them. It told everyone to sit down and put on their seat belts as it tipped back and went straight upward.

One hundred and twenty minutes later they were at the Sea Base, getting off of the Myth inside the R&D hanger. Jack took the Force Generator off the plane and put the new, removable panel back to cover the anchor points for the Force Generator. R&D decided that they used it enough they didn't want miscellaneous holes drilled in the frame of the aircraft. The cover even had a Military part number.

Christi turned off her Force Generator only to have Mark turn it back on for her. He looked at her, "Not until you are inside our part of the Sea Base. The demons can drop in here if they want to."

Christi swatted her forehead with the palm of her right hand to indicate that was dumb, she knew better.

CHAPTER NINE

After they had finished their After-Action reports, cleaned up their gear and returned the Force Generators to the vault, the Extraction Team got a chance to take a shower and put on fresh clothes.

Christi walked out of the bedroom in her apartment and came over to Rachel who stood up to greet her. She looked a lot smaller without the body armor, weapons, golden armor and sword, not to mention the Force Generator. Christi put her arms around her and hugged her; and told her, "Welcome to the Crossfire Team's base."

Christi's best friend in the world said "I have so many questions I don't know where to start."

Christi smiled at her and sat down on the couch in her living room. "Maybe I can make it easier for you. Let me tell you all the major things and then you can ask about everything else. Is that all right with you?"

Rachel nodded. Christi told her about her life since she had said goodbye in front of her apartment four weeks ago. She told her about her mission, her training, her battles, the PM's Office, and the life she would have to live for the near future. Then she got serious.

"Rachel, I can't tell you how becoming a warrior servant for the true God of the Universe has affected me. I have had a complete paradigm shift concerning the importance of living for Yahveh and his Son Yahshua. I thought I was spiritually correct, but sadly, I not only missed the boat, I didn't even know it existed. I am now on a fast track to doing everything I can to please God. Several problems facing us here. I, and I hope you; will only be here for about three more years. After that, we get to go to heaven and spend eternity with Yahveh and Yahshua. I need for you to understand the reality of God and I pray that you will learn to love him back for all the good things he has done for you since you were born."

"I really thought you knew Yahshua, or Jesus. When that LED on the Force Generator turned red, I was shocked. That changed everything about our rescuing you.

You were, as they say, "In the Wind". But, as it turned out it was for good because we were able to save most of those soldiers from the demons."

Rachel nodded her head. "Okay, I think I understand what you are saying. My concerns are things like, now that you've rescued me to a place of safety from the FBI and the demons, what will I do? I don't think I will be a warrior like you have become and I don't have any real skills I can use in here that I know of. I can't just live off of your Team and do nothing. I guess my acting days are over since "break a leg" in this venue apparently means "break your neck". I can't even go out into the city up there without the threat of death or kidnap, which would be worse. That is my biggest concern. I want to pull my own weight. Doesn't having all these warrior types distract you? It would me."

Christi smiled at her again. "Well, for one thing, both of my brothers are here as SOG warriors. That means Sensitive Operations Group. And they will never let me become involved with a Military type." As far as what you will do for the foreseeable future is something we will pray about. You see, God wants you to have the desires of your heart and that won't include sitting around being useless. Secondly, there are a lot of people our age here and you can make a lot of good friends, both men and women. As a warning, don't get too friendly with the warriors of the Team, some of them have seriously lethal wives, understand?"

Rachel smiled at her. "Okay, how do I get a room and clothes and a toothbrush and other things?"

Christi stood up, "You come with me."

She took Rachel down to the War Room and asked Jack if he had time to talk to them for a bit. He did and they went to an area of the huge Living Area and found some seats together. Jack said, "How can I help you ladies?"

Christi outlined Rachel's concerns and needs and asked Jack how they could take care of that since they couldn't leave the base."

Jack looked at her. "How do you want to handle Rachel's housing?"

Christi realized this was a test of sorts. "She needs a place to live and even though we're best friends we don't do well living in the same space. Also, at the present, my beliefs, my life, and my mission focus are paramount and I think you know that."

Jack smiled, "Okay then, I will discuss it with the staff and we might be able to work out something. For now, I will assign her a two-person room in the SOG area. They are nice rooms but we can do better for you. I will have Ethan Reaper get you the standard package of supplies which will cover about every need from toothpaste to utility clothes, bedding, and personal needs. He can also get her entertainment equipment. We can go on from there." Jack addressed Rachel, "This will get you through the first week. Now I have already prayed and sought God for your destiny and your mission, at least while you're with us. Why don't we pray now and see what God has in store for you? Is that agreeable with you, Rachel?"

Rachel sighed, "According to the little light on the Force Generator I may not have the prayer skills to do a lot."

Jack laughed and it was contagious and the women also laughed. "Don't worry about that. You will find that praying for answers is an occupation here and you can get all the training you want or need and, most possibly, even more than that. I suggest this time you let us pray and you be in agreement with our prayers. Later you can visit with Laura or myself and learn what you feel you want and need to learn. Mainly, after we pray just rest in the Lord and listen for an answer, a leading, a direction or even a Scripture."

Jack began to praise God and Yahshua and then sang two simple church songs because God inhabits the praise and worship of His people.

Rachel followed Jack's suggestions and let Jack and Christi pray and then she calmed herself like she would before going before the camera or on stage. It was comfortable and soothing to her spirit.

Jack sat up and said, "I got a word from the Lord. I don't expect you got anything as yet. Do you want to hear what God told me?"

Rachel hadn't heard anything, true, but Jack's words struck a chord inside of her that told her that what Jack was going to tell her was true. She nodded his head.

Jack looked at Christi who was smiling. "Did you get anything?"

Christi smiled and said "I did, and since we have the same Elohim I am fairly sure that it will match what you got. Hang on for a second." She was no longer carrying a purse but from her pocket she took out a small notebook and a pen and wrote several lines in it. She tore the paper out and folded it. She passed the paper to Rachel. "Don't read that until after Jack tells you what he got."

Jack looked at Rachel. "The Lord told me that you are not here as a coincidental happening. In fact, in ancient Hebrew there is no word for "coincidence", it is just God working miracles anonymously. You probably are not aware that your spirit came before God when you were created and he gave you a destiny and a mission for Him. You have just reached the beginning of your mission. I am going to offer you a position with the Crossfire Team." Jack saw her frown. "Don't worry, this isn't charity and you will earn your keep but, it isn't combat like you saw today."

Jack smiled at Christi. "Rachel, I want you to become a part of our Security group. Your training and your learning to become an actor was actually God's desire for you to learn how to read and deal with people. In short I am going to offer you a once in a lifetime opportunity to become a spy."

There was a stunned silence for several seconds before Rachel blinked and said. "I'll take it."

Christi looked at Rachel. "You're sure? You only thought about it for a few seconds."

Rachel grinned, "You don't understand. As you know I've played a lot of roles and done a lot of role playing in video games. I've never gotten lost in them because I can see how they could be improved to be more effective. I also have studied the art of spy craft when I had the time. When Jack told me what God had for me to do, it rang a major chord in my spirit." She looked at Jack and reached over and shook his hand. You couldn't have pointed to a bigger desire in my life. Also, it is like stage work but for real."

Jack nodded, "Okay then, I will tell you that it will involve lots of hours with several of our real life spies and you are going to have to get in shape, learn how to handle all sorts of weapons, learn some Martial Arts, As I told you, it won't be full combat but you will be around nefarious types and you will need to defend yourself."

Rachael took on a somber tone and nodded her head. She felt a thrill about her future that acting had never given her before,

Jack said, "Okay then, I'll work up your paperwork and you can sign it tomorrow. I'll let Christi tell you all about the pay and benefits because I just told her about them two weeks ago. Now, understand this, this position is one of critical importance to the Team. After your training you will return to us here. You will have a lot of responsibility, but we are a team. You'll also have backup and help, both of the earthly type and Angelic also."

Jack and Rachel stood up at the same time. "Welcome aboard, Rachel. You get a day or so to rest up and then I'll have Sarah make up a schedule for you. In fact, she will be one of your instructors."

Rachel asked Christi, "Why Sarah?"

Christi and Jack both laughed. Christi took Rachel's hands. "Sarah is a former Israeli Mossad Field Agent and Assassin. You couldn't ask for a better person to teach you spy craft. She taught Jack, Laura, myself, and most of the others here. She is good. And she doesn't fill it out by herself. David Zahavy was Sarah's boss at the Mossad and a legend in the spy world. There is also Alexis Zahavy. Yes, she is David Zahavy's wife. And if you want to see deadly action, you need to watch them work as a team."

CHAPTER TEN

That night as she lay in her new bed, Rachel's head was spinning at her fortune and the myriad of things she had to remember. She thought, "And I'm not even in class yet!"

Christi was lying on her stomach on her bed with her room set to invisible. She was floating serenely on the Mediterranean Sea. The temperature was perfect and there were only little waves and best of all, there were no insects at all. She thought about her day. "I started out as an American with an unknown mission who was depending on my relatives to validate me with the Team. Now, I am an Israeli with a still unknown mission but with the entire Team's survival is dependent on me. My best friend has been hired by the Team to an important position, a James Bond spy job no less." She closed her eyes and thanked the Creator of the Universe for all of her good fortune and future. She prayed with her whole heart and soul.

Back in her room Rachel remembered the piece of paper Christi had given her. She rolled over and pulled the piece of paper out of her pocket. She unfolded it and read:

Rachel, you are going to be working for the Crossfire Team as a spy. Congratulations, Christi.

She thought about the identical information Jack had given her. "Maybe that was their plan all along and God didn't have anything to do with it. Drat!"She'd actually believed that it was a mission from God. As she sat there she heard a voice, a very masculine voice, one very close to her. She looked around and found a powerful man sitting on the end of her bed. Rachel wondered how he got into her bedroom, she'd locked her door. Maybe this guy had another key.

"What do you want?"Rachel asked

"My name is Raquel and I am concerned about your stubborn lack of faith."

Rachel was getting upset. "You don't know what my faith is and you don't have a right to be in my room." She was somewhat frightened yet, at the same time attracted to the big man. She thought, "What would Christi think if she knew he was here."

Raquel sighed. "Alright, you want to do this the hard way." He made a gesture and he was sitting on nothing and Rachel was lying on the ground in her sleeping gown she had fashioned from a large T-shirt and her underwear. Rachel looked around, but because she didn't have her glasses, everything was blurry. Raquel touched Rachel's head and suddenly everything was clear as a bell in all directions and at all distances. She couldn't believe the beauty she was seeing everywhere. "Where...Where are we?"

Raquel said, "You are in one area of Heaven in the future. Look over there, here comes someone you knew in the past."

Rachel looked up and rose up into a seating position. A woman in her thirties was walking up to her. Rachel sort of recognized the woman but she wasn't sure. The woman stopped near her and smiled, "Hello Rachel, I'm glad to see you again. You are looking wonderful. You've turned out to be a beautiful young woman. You make me one very proud Grandmother. I know you're not staying here this trip. I'll be looking forward to seeing you soon. We can peel potatoes and talk about everything like we used to do in my kitchen. Bye for now." She walked casually away. Rachel noticed how happy she was and the fact that she had both legs again.

Rachel felt that she had been hit in the stomach. Her Granny and she used to peel potatoes in the springtime.

Raquel said, "Here is another of your friends."

Rachel looked and didn't see any people but something came rushing up to her and jumped into her lap and started licking her face. She grabbed the little dog and really got choked up. It was "Petey" her truest friend and her rock in rough times. When I was eight years old, he died. That was nineteen years ago. Petey licked Rachel's hand and then scampered off.

Rachel stared at Raquel, "How did you get him here?"

Raquel smiled, "I didn't get him here. He lives here and he came because he knew you'd be here. Is there anyone else you have lost, that knew the Lord Yahshua or Jesus that you would like to see?"

Rachel thought back. "When I was seventeen and in high school, my best and probably only, boyfriend at that time, Charlie Elkhoen, was killed in a car wreck with his parents. I missed him for several years. In fact, I still miss him."

Raquel told Rachel, "Wait a few minutes."

As she waited Rachel realized that the aromas from the plants and the grass were, well, Heavenly. Her soul soaked up the ambience of the place which filled her with peace. A man in his young thirties walked up to Rachel. It didn't take Rachel a great effort to see it was Charlie a few years older but still the same. She got up and hugged him and held him out at arm's length and stared at him in happiness. "You are a sight to see. Boy! I've missed you so much for so long. Are you really happy here?"

Charlie smiled at Rachel. "I'm so much more than happy, sunshine girl." Sunshine girl was the name that Charlie always called her when they lived on Earth. "I am greatly satisfied and I apologize for leaving you when I did. I know I didn't have anything to say about it. But, I knew you'd miss me and there wasn't anything I could do about it. I am so glad to have this chance to see you and I hope you'll be coming back here soon, so we can hang together again. I want you to know that I still love you. Always have. I'm really looking forward to seeing you again, soon. Bye Rachel."

Rachel turned to Raquel. "Thank you for letting me see my relatives and friends who left Earth too early. Why are you doing this?"

Raquel looked at Rachel. "Because Jack and Laura Malone are my fellow warriors and I honor their friendship greatly. Plus, I am beginning to share that feeling with Christi. I don't want them to be hurt and disappointed by you because you are too stubborn and blind to see the truth of God and His Son, Yahshua. You have had many chances to give your life to Jesus as Christi has, but you let your intelligence contradict what your heart is telling you about the truth. Beware, Satan has a hold on you and he will lead you away from this." Raquel spread his arms out to encompass all of Heaven. If you want, I can remove the stronghold Satan established in you to harden your heart twenty-nine years ago and let the truth set you free."

Rachel stood there in her sleep shirt and underwear and thought about Raquel's offer. She looked up, "You're an Angel of God, right?"

Raquel nodded his head and his blonde hair swirled around his head. "I am an Angel of God."

Rachel took a deep breath. "Okay, Raquel, I am asking you of my own volition to remove any and all strongholds or whatever they're called and any other hindrance Satan has burdened me with and seal my life so that he can never do that to me again."

Raquel looked at Rachel for less than fifteen seconds. "All right, you are free and have the right to accept Yahveh or not as you please. The right to choose is yours."

Rachel was amazed that it would be that easy. She decided to test Raquel's cleansing of her body, soul, and spirit. She got down on her knees and prayed that if Jesus is real that He would tell her that He was the Savior of all mankind." She knelt there and realized her heart was crying out that God would prove that He was real. It suddenly was so important that Rachel knew she could not go on if it wasn't true.

Raquel got down on one knee and bowed his head as a brilliant, but not blinding, light covered Rachel. Yahshua stood before her. *"Rachel Reynolds, open your eyes and open your heart."* As Rachel opened her eyes she knew the Savior of the World stood before her. Her whole body gave proof of that fact. Now that she wasn't blinded and doubtful she said, "Thank you my God. I am so sorry that I doubted you for so long and that I had the audacity to test you. Forgive me my sins because I am a sinner. I can't tell you how much I love you. I always have but I didn't let myself know it."

Yahshua took Rachel's arm and lifted her to her feet. The Savior pulled her into His embrace. Rachel's tears fell like rivers. Eventually she stepped back and looked at her King with eyes that were full of love. Yahshua smiled at her, *"Welcome to the Kingdom of Heaven Rachel Reynolds. You will do great things for me and for your fellow man. Remember, I love you with a love that is never ending."*

Rachel came back to awareness in her room, alone. She didn't doubt what happened for a second. She got down on her knees and prayed a grateful heart to a Savior that heard her. Jumping up she felt she was King of the world too. She grabbed her cell phone and typed out a text to Christi, telling her that she had gone to Heaven and met Yahshua and gave her life to the Savior and she couldn't wait to yell it from the highest hill.

She sat there and realized she no longer had the discouragement she once had for, well, forever. She was full of hope and energy and the whole world was in front of her.

Her phone chirped and she read Christi's return text. "Rachel, I am thrilled for you. This has taken a weight off of me that has bothered me for a long time. As my very best friend I want to tell you that you are now going to spend eternity as my sister with me in heaven. That's wonderful news, even if it is 4:00 A.M."

Rachel finally laid down to rest and immediately fell into a sweet sleep.

CHAPTER ELEVEN

Rachel was up before 8:00 A.M. and she went to the main floor and walked up to the door to the War Room. At least she was pretty sure that was what Christi called it.

She stood in the doorway and looked around at the futuristic command and control center for the Crossfire Team. She was fascinated by the communications systems and was definitely gawking when someone pushed her into the room from behind. She turned around to find Mark Connelly standing there looking at her. Mark said, "I know you're not lost and I know you want something, so come in and ask."

Rachel stepped further into the War Room. "This looks great. I do have a request though. Could you help me get one of the Force Generator thingies and let me try it on today?"

Mark looked at the young woman and realized there was something about her that was different. No, there were two things that were different. The first was, she had a different attitude and a much happier spirit. The second was that she wasn't wearing her glasses. "Did you switch to contacts?"

Rachel's hand raced up to her face and she smiled a big smile at Mark. "WOW! I've had to wear glasses since I was four years old. The Angel Raquel touched my face last night and I can see perfectly now. I didn't even realize I didn't have my glasses."

Mark had an idea of what happened last night. So he told Rachel to come with him. They went to the vault in the Armory and Mark got one of the Force Generator belt units out and tested it. It worked fine for him. He gave it to Rachel who strapped it on and confidently threw the switch. The LED glowed a solid green this time. Rachel jumped up and yelled, "Yes!"She turned it off and gave it back to Mark. "Thank you Mark, so much."

Mark put the Force Generator back in the vault and locked it shut. He smiled at Rachel, "Make a serious commitment last night?"

Rachel almost talked Mark's leg off describing what happened in the night time.

Mark grinned, "So the Angel Raquel gave you the tour of Heaven did he?"Rachel nodded her head while grinning like a child in a candy store with an unlimited credit card. Mark laughed, "Congratulations and welcome sister. You couldn't have been too stubborn. That's when Raquel gives you the tour of hell."

Rachel's eyes got big, "Really?" Mark nodded as they reached the War Room again. As he was about to enter he looked at Rachel. "You need to talk to Jack or Laura about last night. Oh! And by the way, Raquel is not just an Angel of God; He's an Archangel." He left Rachel standing there with her mouth open.

Later that morning, Christi and Rachel came into the War Room and asked Jack if he had another moment to talk to them. Jack looked at the young women and shook his head. "I have to leave in about fifteen minutes for a meeting in Tel Aviv. What is the subject you need to discuss?"

Christi looked at him, "It's about the way you pray, we don't understand it."

Jack smiled, "I'll tell Laura to help you. She is our spiritual leader and the first one to pray in any and all circumstances. Let me call her."

Ten minutes later Christi and Rachel met Laura in a small conference room off of the Living Area.

Laura took the far side of the conference table and sat in one chair and put her feet up in another chair. "What can I help you guys with?"

Rachel said, "When Jack prays he refers to the seven places that Yahshua shed his blood. I thought one just said "in the blood Jesus shed at Calvary". What are the seven places and why is it important to mention all of them?"

Laura looked at them for a few seconds. "The reason we specify the seven places is because it is important to refer to the precise blood you are pleading so that it is effective. We have been studying the Jewish Roots of Jesus and we are finding that God is much more moved by many things the Jewish people have been doing for centuries. You know the saying and the song, "The Power is in the Blood?"

They both nodded. Laura smiled, "Then the power is in the correct blood the Savior shed for a specific need in our lives. The Torah Scroll reminds us that God's commandments are the pathway to life. The 7 drops of blood on the mezuzahs on our doorposts symbolize the seven places Jesus shed His blood. They remind us that we have been redeemed by His Blood in every area of life."

"The seven places that Jesus shed His blood for us are as follows:"

"Number one: Jesus sweated blood in the Garden of Gethsemane - this was to redeem our will. Remember that Adam had done his own thing in the Garden of Eden, essentially saying, "Not your will Father, but my will. This gave the keys to the Earth and our will to Satan. Well, Jesus got the keys to the Earth back from Satan by defeating Satan at the cross and He redeemed our wills by shedding his blood over the issue of whose will is in charge at the Garden of Gethsemane. We are no longer slaves to Satan, we have our wills back."

"Number two: "Jesus gave us healing by shedding His Blood at the Whipping Post. "By His Stripes we are healed." Jesus gave us spiritual healing and freedom from Sickness by shedding His Blood for us at the Whipping Post."

"Number three: Jesus shed His Blood on the Crown of Thorns. This was to break the curse of poverty. When God threw Adam and Eve out of the Garden of Eden he told Adam that He (God) would no longer be mankind's provider and that Adam would earn his living tilling the ground and God cursed mankind by making the ground produce "thorns and thistles". When the Roman soldiers made a "Crown of Thorns" and pushed it into Jesus forehead and He bled, He replaced the "sweat" from Adam's brow with the blood from His brow. That blood broke the curse of poverty."

"Number four: The Nails that pierced His Hands were to restore our Dominion and bless the works of our hands so that anything we put our hands to prospers."

"Number five: The Nail that pierced his feet restored our authority, which Satan had taken from Adam. Wherever we put our feet we establish our God-given authority."

"Number six: He bled when the Roman guard pierced His side and the blood was mixed with water that showed he had died of a broken heart. This blood was shed to mend the broken hearted."

"Number seven: He bruised His heel when he stomped on Satan's head as prophesied, "Your child will crush Satan's head and he will bruise His heel". He did this to break the power of Iniquity, which is a curse. This is when He took the Keys of Heaven and Earth back from Satan who had stolen them from Adam."

Laura took two long cards out of her brief case. "Here are two cards that repeat what I just told you. Refer to these until you have the seven places memorized. To summarize, if you are praying to break off a curse on yourself or someone else, plead the blood that Yahshua shed by bruising his heel when he stomped on Satan's head and took back the keys of Heaven and Earth. If you are praying for healing you plead the blood Yahshua shed at the whipping post where the saying is; "By my stripes you are healed", and don't forget He said on the cross, "It is finished". He has already answered all your prayers and needs as well as forgiving you of all your sins. You just need to receive it, believe it, and claim it. Here are two DVDs from a Pastor on the subject. They are worth watching."

CHAPTER TWELVE

As they walked back toward Christi's apartment Rachel shook her head, "Boy that was great, I learned a lot. But, there is so much to learn."

Christi nodded her head. "Yeah, but I want to learn everything so I can tell other people about whatever they want to know. I'm going to enroll in Laura's class on religion and spiritual knowledge, how about you?"

Rachel laughed, "I'm already enrolled in that. Hey, Jack asked the Rabbi here to baptize me tonight, will you come and watch?"

Christi thought about that. "I'll come, but I'm not going to just watch." At Rachel's questioning look; she smiled. "I am going to get baptized myself. It's been years since I was baptized and Sarah says we each should be baptized at least once a year. It breaks off all connection to negativity and curses."

Rachel pursed her lips and then smiled, "I like that idea."

That evening the entire Core Team and many of the SOG group were present in support of Christi and Rachel's Baptisms. Rabbi Joshua Epstein officiated at the ceremony. He made sure that both people to be baptized had bathed and prayed about the upcoming baptism. He then explained the ceremony. "I will call each of you into the baptismal pool, one at a time. I will ask you if you have trusted Yahshua or Jesus as your Lord and Savior. After you agree that you have trusted Yahshua as your Lord and Savior I will lower you down into the water until you have been immersed completely. I will then raise you back up immediately."

"Baptism is a public confession of faith in Yahshua but more importantly, it breaks all connection with failure for the past year. It also purifies your spirit in the eyes of Yahveh. You may experience a clearer contact with God and also you'll have an improvement in your spiritual understanding of the Bible and your life in Christ."

"Since Rachel requested Baptism first, I call her to join me in the Baptismal pool."Rachel went down the seven steps into the water and stood next to Rabbi Epstein.

The Rabbi asked her about her faith and dependence in Yahshua. Rachel said, "I believe in Yahshua as my Lord and Savior and need Him in everything I do." The Rabbi leaned her over backward and immersed her. He lifted Rachel back up and gave her a hug to the cheers and applause of the attending warriors. He repeated the ceremony with Christi. After Rachel and Christi changed clothes and cleaned up, they walked out of the changing rooms and were mobbed by the others and ended up hugging everyone, at least once.

Laura discussed having a new members meeting party, but Jack vetoed that idea for now. "We've got a situation coming up that takes precedence over social matters. I just got a call from General Levy that one of their nonexistent nuclear sites is under attack from an unknown group, and there are demons involved."

Mark frowned, "The question is; is this attempt to really steal another nuke or is this trap for us?"

Jack shook his head. "It doesn't matter either way. We need to handle the demonic angle."

Mark grinned, "Well, I know that the attackers are not going to get another nuke. As soon as an alarm is sounded, all of the nuclear bombs and missiles are automatically moved into vaults that can't be penetrated. Even if the attackers overrun the base they can't get to the nuclear stuff."

Jack held up his left hand fingers up. He folded one finger for each exception. "One, not unless there are bombs or missiles in maintenance. Two, not unless there are missiles or bombs in transit but still on the base. Three, not unless the attackers can jam the vault operation. Four, not unless they have inside help. Five, anything else that the devil can devise."

Mark made a sour face. "Yeah, there is that." He keyed his battle/COMM. "All hands, combat alert, gear up with FGs and meet on the airfield in ten minutes. Su Li, Mike White, two Chinooks hot in fifteen minutes, use Mossad Flight Contact. MC out."

He thought for a few seconds. Then he keyed the communications again. "Christi, with me, Carol, Sniper gear, Ethan, local COMM/SEC control, Elon with Jack. MC out."

Jack looked at Mark, "FG? MC?"

Mark nodded, "FG is shorthand for Force Generators and I like to think of MC as "Master of Ceremonies" but it's just my initials for identification."

Jack nodded, "Okay, but get me a list of these shorthand names. What are mine and Laura's shorthand names?

Mark put on his helmet. "Don't you read your email? I put it in your email box three days ago. Yours is JM and Laura's is LM or course. I was going to give Sarah HT for Holy Terror but I relented before I proved it to myself. Hers is SC." The three of them ran for the airfield.

The two Chinooks, two-rotor transport helicopters were sitting on the tarmac already warmed up with their dual rotors spinning. Mark took thirteen warriors with him and Jack took the other thirteen with him. They were loaded and airborne in less than five minutes.

Su Li called Mark to the flight deck. "What's the drill this time, General?"

Mark stood in the cockpit doorway. "The usual, demons, nuclear weapons, probably a trap for us. Set us down inside the base wire, fifty feet from where Mike sets down. Shut these down and join us for the festivities."

Su Li grinned, "Yes Sir, General, will do." She keyed her comm and got Mike and gave him the orders.

Mark kneeled down next to Ethan Reaper. "Show me the latest on the Nuke Site."

Ethan laid his large Tablet display so Mark could see it. Ethan had a double audio input in his left ear and a different one in his right ear. His microphone auto switched to the active channel. "The battle is nip and tuck for the Israelis due to the demons." He pointed out the weak spots and Mark assigned the different squads to targets on either side of their landing places.

Mark coordinated with the Mossad and the IDF to make sure the local troops knew that the Crossfire Team was going to be there in six minutes and they were not the enemy.

A minute later the Base Commander made contact with Mark. "You will be a welcome addition to our little war here Mark. This is Major Kravitz; I met you at the PMs Office the other day when you dispatched those three demons. A short sit rep. We have them blocked from three of the five entrances and we have an active fire watch on the rest of the perimeter. All, and I mean all, of the weapons are in lock down but they keep pushing to get into the storage area. We've taken out over fifty of their human warriors but we can't hurt the demons. I'll meet you as you land. Oh, I see you now. I will meet you in a few minutes, Kravitz out."

Mark had a catch in his spirit. He called his IDF contact. "What is the Base Commander's name and does he lead from the front?"

Captain Benny Horvitz, the contact, replied, "The Base Commanders name is Kravitz and he did lead from the front, but he was killed twenty minutes ago."

Mark sighed, "Who is in charge now?"

"A Captain Lowen, if he has survived so far."

Mark hit the All-Hands key on his battle/COMM. "Beware, the demons are impersonating base personnel. The base commander, Major Kravitz was killed twenty-five minutes ago and just called me to tell me that he would meet me when we land in two minutes. It will be a disguised demon. I will handle it but there could be more demons disguised as humans, MC out."

The Chinooks sat down at the same time and the warriors had their FGs on and they fanned out and advanced on the two weaker areas on the base.

The fake Base Commander, Major Horowitz ran over to him and said, "General Connelly?" Mark's armor and sword were already in place and, with one stroke, he beheaded the fake Horowitz. Mark kept moving as the demon dissolved into red smoke and demon stain. Suddenly, dozens of demons flooded out of a new rift and attacked the Crossfire Team warriors with all the ferocity they could muster, which was an enormous amount. Three missiles slammed into the mass of demons as they exited the rift ran toward the Team members. These missiles were able to eliminate all the illegal demons.

Dozens of demons died but three times that many survived and kept attacking the Force Generator fields to no avail. Jack assigned Laura and a team of five to move on the entrances and clear out the gate area and work their way back out. He and the other ten Team members worked to eliminate all the demons they could. Mark's command was doing the same. The area was soon fogged over in various colors of smoke and the ground covered in demon stain. For Jack, the chore of dispatching demons did not become boring just because the demons couldn't hurt them. He saw it as a great time to refine his sword techniques so that when the time came that they couldn't use the Force Generators he would be more effective.

As for the demons, Jack had found four that responded to the code word and allowed God to change their lives and minds. He allowed them to leave the field of battle and return to the rift. This would enlarge the rebellion against Satan and increase the light in the demonic dimension.

Regardless what the demons threw against the Team nothing affected them. They just kept cutting down demons at a tremendous rate. They had been reaping the field for over an hour when all the remaining demons disappeared suddenly and the rift snapped closed.

Mark's voice reminded everyone to stay on guard and leave the FGs on in the event this was a trick to make them let their guard down.

Nineteen humans that had been attacking the base with the demons gave up after seeing the demons leave the field of battle. Jack tested each one personally to ensure they were human and not demons. He then had them stripped naked except for their underwear and shackled hand and foot. He left them outside the building on their faces on the ground with five warriors watching them.

He walked into the base and met Mark and Captain Lowen discussing the loss of personnel and damage to the base. As they talked, Su Li called Mark. "There are about two hundred IDF troops outside the base and I am keeping them there until you authorize them to enter. The detachment Commander is very upset and he is demanding that I let them in to help defend the base.

Mark walked out to where Su Li was holding the fort. He stopped by the gate where the five-foot, four-inch Asian female stood alone against a six-foot muscular Major with over two hundred armed Israeli troops. Somehow, in her body armor with her rifle, Su Li looked quite comfortable and quite able to handle the situation.

Mark said, "Commander, I am General Mark Connelly of the Crossfire Team and the reason we are not allowing you in as yet is because the demons have begun to imitate IDF personnel and we have to vet you and your troops first."

The Commander sneered at Mark, "General? In what world and in who's Military are you a General?"

Mark was about to respond when a voice he knew answered for him. "General Mark Connelly is a full, two-star General in the IDF. You would know that if you would take the time to check your messages instead of shining your Major's insignia. I advise you to wipe that sneer off of your face, apologize to General Connelly, and treat him with the proper respect a superior officer deserves. Is that clear?"

The Major was literally shaking in his boots in front of General Levy. "Yes Sir!" He turned to Mark, "I am sorry I acted disrespectfully, Sir.

Mark nodded and turned to General Levy. "Thank you, General. Normally I would have each man tested to see if our armor appears. But, in the interest of time I will take a quicker way. Raquel!"

The Archangel appeared two feet off of the ground in his Angelic form. He looked absolutely awesome and the wrath of God was on his face. There were cries and fearful yells from the new Israeli IDF forces. The IDF Major was thoroughly convicted of his shortcomings and hung his head.

Mark smiled at Raquel, "Sorry to bother you, but I need your help. Can you scan these troops and let me know if any of them are demons?"

Raquel looked out over the massed men and women. He turned to Mark and General Levy. "All of these are human, except for four of them. I will handle them."

He moved so fast it seemed like he disappeared from in front of Mark and appeared over a part of the crowd with no passage of time. He dropped to the ground with everyone backing up to give him room. He had his sword with the Esteem of Yahveh rolling off of the blade in his hand and he beheaded four soldiers before they could defend themselves.

Some of the soldiers aimed their rifles at the Archangel but dropped the barrels when the four "soldiers" started turning into smoke and demon stain. Raquel immediately returned to where Mark and now Jack were standing with General Levy. "The rest of these men and women are normal human IDF soldiers." Then he disappeared.

General Levy shook Mark's hand, "Thank you again General Connelly. Mark nodded as Su Li stood aside and the troops streamed into the base leaving the four dark stains on the ground.

CHAPTER THIRTEEN

Jack and Mark called the Crossfire Team troops together at the helicopters. While Su Li and Mike looked the helicopters over for damage, Jack asked everyone if there was anything exceptional this time. Craig Steele spoke up, "There was a junk load of demons this time. I think I made Ace."

Mark looked at the former Marine specialist. "Does that mean you killed five demons?"

Craig shook his head, "No, fifty demons."

Sarah shook her head. "If every one of our troops killed fifty demons that means we terminated over seventeen hundred demons in less than one hour."

One of the other troops raised their hand. "Sirs, I was fighting one of the four-legged demons and I'm fairly sure it had a camera, sort of looked like ours do, on its shoulder. But, after I killed the demon, the camera dissolved just like the demon."

Charlie walked up to the front of the assembly. "It could be that the demonic is trying to get a look at our fighting styles or our equipment."

Mark thought about that concept. "We need to look into this, later."

About then General Levy walked up. "You might as well head back to your base. These people here give you their extreme gratitude for your service and will not hesitate to call you if more demons appear here again."

Jack and Mark got everyone back on the choppers and they were able to fly back directly to the base without having to time out any satellites.

Several of the troops cleaned up and finished their After-Action reports and reported to the kitchen to fix dinner for everyone.

Mark was impressed that everyone was learning their Jewish Roots and listening to Rabbi Epstein describe the concepts behind the Torah lessons well enough that they were looking for any chance to bless others so that they could receive a blessing from God.

Mark offered a concept to Jack and they discussed it at length. Eventually, they brought the entire Core Team into the discussion. Finally, after a late hour summation, they prayed to God concerning the idea. No words, no Angels, no Heavenly chorus, just a peace resulted as an answer.

Jack took a vote and declared the idea sound and made an extremely secure phone call. He turned and looked at the assembled crew. "Okay, the solution is available, who goes?"

Everybody in the room held up their hands. Mark wrote down the list. It included; Jack, Laura, Mark himself, Sarah, David, Alexis, Su Li, Mike, Ethan, Elon, Carol, Christi. He decided they needed seven people on this mission. So, he deselected himself, Sarah, Su Li, Elon and Carol. Jack looked at the time. It was a little after 2:26 a.m.

Jack called the R&D group. The phone was answered at this early hour by Captain Maxwell. "Captain, I need to talk to you as soon as you are available."

Captain Maxwell realized that there was some urgency in the request. Therefore, since he was up working late, he appeared at the door to the War Room ten minutes later.

Jack invited him in and gave him a seat that had been vacated by Mark. "Captain, on the last two flights to the U.S., the Myth was detected by the U.S. Air Force or the FBI. This is despite its radar-agile configuration and the fact that it was invisible to normal sight. I believe it could be its heat signature that gave it away. What do you think?"

Captain Maxwell thought about the problem. "Yes, that is possible. When you fly at hyper-sonic speeds at lower altitudes the outer shell of the aircraft develops an extremely high heat radiation. Even slowing down doesn't allow the body to lose enough heat not to be detectable to sensitive thermal gear for quite some time."

Mark asked, "With that heat load it must stand out like a red-hot bullet to any thermal sensing gear on our satellites."

Captain Maxwell shook his head. "No, while the Myth, or the Ghost for that matter, is above 105,600 feet altitude, or twenty miles straight up, they are essentially in space. There are too few molecules of oxygen or other elements to build that type of heat. It is when it drops into the real atmosphere that the heat climbs. Remember the old Space Shuttle programs? Think of a returning space shuttle which had to have ceramic tiles to dissipate the heat created by collisions of the shuttle with air molecules. The speed of the shuttle returning from space causes tremendous heat buildup and even a fire halo. The Myth doesn't heat up like a shuttle but it generates a large heat signature. If it flies in lower altitudes or after being superheated by re-entry it will be detectable until the heat dissipates."

Mark thought about that, "Does the Myth have the ability to monitor thermal emissions?"

Captain Maxwell laughed, "Of course it does, just ask for heat stats and it will give you perceived heat from the outside, internal, and foreseeable future heat levels; depending on speed, altitude, and requested changes.

"So, I can request the Myth to use emitted heat as one of the criteria and it will prevent our being seen due to thermal emissions?

The Captain had been running the problem on his tablet computer and discovered some new information. "Hold on General, I think I've found how they are tagging you so that they can intercept you. For some reason I still get R&D updates from the U.S. It's probably because we were a black ops program. They may not know we're no longer in the U.S. or under their control. Or this could be disinformation although it looks genuine this time.

The USAF Research is running parallel programs and they have an imbedded circuit that is probably responding to a signal from interceptor aircraft or satellites. It was designed to prevent friendly fire attacks. I will see if that was part of the original wiring in the Ghost and Myth airframes. If it is, I will get it removed for all our aircraft."

Mark had a thought. "Do you have anything smaller but just as capable as the Myth or the Ghost? We need something that will handle six to twelve passengers rather than thirty or forty."

Captain Maxwell paused for a few seconds. "Yes, we do. I just didn't think you needed something that small."

Mark smiled, "What are its capabilities?"

The Captain punched up the new aircraft on his screen. "The "Figment" has the same capabilities as the "Myth" but is faster and harder to detect because of its smaller size and footprint. Its engines and electronics are a generation newer and more capable than those in the Myth or the Ghost. I'll get that responder circuitry removed and it'll be ready by tomorrow."

Mark thought a sneaky thought. "Okay, but be careful removing that IFF responder circuit. If I were building a circuit like that into something, I would design it so that if there was any form of failure there would be a backup and a sort of panic transmission about the failure of the responder circuit."

Captain Maxwell caught that thought right away. "I'll have the techs check for that too. Listen; if you ever want a change of duty I could use a mind like yours in design."

Mark laughed, "I'll keep that in mind, Captain. By the way, how many aircraft do you have in R&D?"

"Right now we have thirty-six different air frame types and twenty-four different aircraft. Why?"

"Curiosity mostly, but just in case, a different requirement arises that a different vehicle could give us an advantage."

CHAPTER FOURTEEN

The next morning, the seven-person team walked over to the R&D hanger and was introduced to the "Figment". It looked like a smaller version of the Myth.

Captain Maxwell met them at the hanger door and walked them over to the small aircraft. It was a lifting body with minimal surfaces for a tail or wings. It actually looked mean or threatening due to its configuration.

Jack asked the Captain, "If you are no longer part of the U.S. Air Force how can you get a "newer" generation of aircraft? I mean, the Air Force isn't sending you things like their latest versions are they?"

The Captain smiled, "No, they aren't sending us anything anymore, General Malone. We are working with the Israeli Air Force. They have an equally aggressive program of R&D that is on the leading edge of aircraft development that includes the latest development from the U.S. programs. Let's say that the Israelis are in on all the latest black ops programs in the U.S., China, Russia, and Sweden. This isn't a known or legal arrangement but it is very efficient."

Jack shook the Captain's hand and climbed on board the smaller aircraft which was longer, a little wider, and about the same height as the Shrews that the Crossfire Team owned. Jack found the same cover panel next to the door and placed a Force Generator in the connection studs. He activated the "special" mode and to the outside, the Figment disappeared.

All though there were only twelve seats, three sets of two seats on either side of the aisle, the seats wore spacious and comfortable. The large information and view screen at the front of the craft were comparable to those in the Myth. Jack connected his tablet computer to the aircraft electronics at a receptacle in the arm rest at his seat and then added the thermal emissions to the list of desired characteristics to prevent detection by satellite or ground stations. The trip to the U.S. was even faster than the Myth due to the smaller weight requirements and the newer engine designs. The trip to the surface took longer while the Figment slowed to shed detectable heat to an acceptable level. The Figment settled to the ground undetected near an unused ski area almost a hundred miles west of Denver, Colorado and under the cover of a large covered parking lot that was almost empty.

Jack switched the FG to "normal" and the plane appeared. There was a pair of large 4x4 pickup trucks already parked under the roof of the parking lot.

Dr. Clashire and several techs got out of the trucks and came over and looked at the Figment in awe. The side door opened and the team deplaned.

Jack shook hands with Dr. Clashire. They made the switch of several large packages from the backs of the trucks to the aircraft storage bay behind the seats and then everyone got on the Figment and Jack rendered it invisible again.

Everyone sat around in a circle or in the seats as they discussed what they were doing. Laura and Christi had raided the small galley and gotten soft drinks or orange juice for everyone.

Jack looked at the Doctor. "Tell me what you've come up with for us Doctor Clashire."

The Doctor smiled. "Well, with all thanks and praise to Yahveh we have again exceeded your requests. In those bundles there are another thirty-one body armor packages with built-in Force Generators. They also have a new version of video cameras. It took a lot of prayer and supplication to God but these cameras, working through the Force Generators have greatly improved optics, lenses and software. Not only will you be able to see everything about your demonic enemies but you can record it also."

For the seven people from Israel this was incredible. Jack said, "I thought it was impossible to record spiritual beings or even capture them with video cameras."

Doctor Clashire nodded his head in agreement. "It is normally impossible to record an Angelic or demonic spirit. It requires an active human mind to see them. But, this is not so when they are in a created body. Which they have to do to interact physically with humans. Then they can be recorded, if you do it God's way. That is why only the cameras attached to the FGs can do it. The FGs are literally a form of God's Holy Spirit power and that is what allows us to record the created body."

"After it is recorded, you can transfer the images just like a normal image. What you can't do is go any further with the image. If the image captured by the camera connected to the FG is copied that is the end of the line for that image. You can't re-record it, share it, or do anything with it. It is like it has an aura on it and it won't allow the image to be used for broadcast or distribution. But, it should help Mr. Reaper in creating his files of demons. His files can only be viewed by a human, not by a mechanism such as a printer."

Jack smiled, "That is okay, we'll take that much. Why did you say it took a lot of prayer?"

"Because God had to make a special dispensation to allow the recording and one-time transfer from the camera storage to a selected media. If someone were to steal one of these new Body Armor/FGs from you, there could be pictures on the camera memory, they will never see them. God's rules will also destroy the FGs in the body armor in less than twenty-four hours. How it knows that it is no longer in your hands is mathematics way beyond my knowledge."

CHAPTER FIFTEEN

Jack prayed for the blessings of Yahveh God over the Doctor and all of his people. They were just about to get up and leave when the Figment announced, "There are other people in the garage. Facial recognition identifies three of the five people as FBI Agents. The other two people are U.S. Military, spec ops personnel."

The five men were sneaking up on the two trucks and didn't seem to know that the Figment was there. Jack saw one of the men heading on a path that would have him walk into the invisible plane in the next ten steps.

Jack asked, "Is there a phone in the truck?"

Dr. Clashire didn't know but one of the techs did. "Yes Sir, here is the number. He read off the number while Jack dialed it. Jack said out loud. "Exterior Audio On".

They could suddenly hear the muffled footsteps of the men and the sudden ringing of the cell phone.

All five of the men ran to the lead truck with their weapons out and trained on the truck. They opened the truck door and found the phone. One of the FBI types picked it up and pushed "answer". Jack said, "When are you government types going to learn to leave us alone?"

While the FBI Agent formulated an answer, Jack told the Figment to stun all five men. There was a buzzing sound outside the plane and all five men crumpled to the floor of the garage. Jack said, "Complete frequency block for a distance of two hundred feet including cell phone frequencies."

Jack switched the FG on the plane to "normal" and opened the outside door. They gathered up the five men and set them on some benches that were chained to the building for use next season. The locals got in the trucks after saying goodbye and drove out of the garage and onto the road to the Interstate back to Denver.

Ethan walked back to the Figment and smiled. "I scrubbed the memories in their cameras and replaced them with a picture of Yahshua in the clouds in power."

After everyone was aboard, the Figment blinked out and became invisible. It lifted up off of the floor of the garage and slid out from under the roof of the garage. It rose fairly slowly until it reached the edge of space and then headed back to Israel, undetected.

An hour after the entire team had returned to the Crossfire portion of the Sea Base, Jack called the Core Team into the War Room. When everyone was settled Jack told them about the new FG/Body Armor. "This new combination eliminates the need to strap on a FG. This will confuse and mislead the demons. The addition of the new cameras will give us a much better view of our combat capabilities and allow us to correct any tendencies to prevent making a pattern out of bad techniques. With the exception of three specific use models, the older FGs are non-functional and will be destroyed per God's Commandments."

He looked over the assembled cast of characters. "Since everyone needs to have their body armor available at all times you will be assigned one of the new FG/B models. You will keep it with you or handy. Be aware that if anyone other than the owner tries to use or take your armor, the FG portion of the armor will not function, even if they are one of the Team. I highly recommend that two of you don't mix up your armors. This responsibility is yours and you should honor God by protecting it and preventing the other person or both of you from being cursed by God."

Jack, Laura, Mark, and Sarah prayed for wisdom in the matter of destroying the first models of the FGs. God was specific in His commandment. "You shall melt the units until there is no atomic structure remaining." It was clear, concise, and pointed. Jack counted the units on the trolley. There were exactly forty-three units. He had Mark double check the count. The four Team members closed the housing on the trolley and guided the trolley out of the Armory and to the R&D Laboratory.

Laura and then Sarah counted the units placed into the electronic arc furnace. The furnace was activated and all four members watched as the forty-three Force Generators were melted down to liquid and the liquid was reduced to a mist. The mist underwent stringent tests that verified the mass of the mist equaled the mass of the original units.

The mist was allowed to cool and condense into a pool at the bottom of the furnace. That was subjected to an even more intense heat through the electronic arc that reduced the pool to sub molecular liquid. That was also cooled and coalesced and mixed with an acid that destroyed the molecular liquid until there was nothing, not even ash.

Jack nodded his head and the four members knelt and prayed in submission to the Father and prayed that all they had done was as commanded. A peace came over all four of them. They rose and thanked the metal workers in the R&D lab for their assistance.

CHAPTER SIXTEEN

On the way back to the Armory with the empty trolley following faithfully along behind them, Sarah asked Jack, "I understand that God ordered us to destroy them and how much he wanted to make sure they were completely destroyed. What I don't understand is that the units were completely useless unless the Father powered them. Why did they have to be completely obliterated?"

Jack smiled, "Because the Father said to do it that way. I don't understand the basics of how they even work, but that doesn't matter. You are enough of a mature Messianic Jew to know that our understanding is not required. We are servants and we serve. We don't have to be told the details because we probably couldn't understand the need to do it that way. God does understand it and He is a loving God, the end."

As they neared the entrance to the Crossfire Team part of the base, they met Christi, Su Li, Carol, and Alexis coming out of the base toward them.

From the look of seriousness on their faces all four of the Senior Team members reached up and activated their FGs. Jack asked, "What's the problem?"

Christi sighed, "I got a message on my cell phone ten minutes ago. A very ghoulish voice told me to tell Jack, that they have the Director of the Mossad and they want to discuss an arrangement to trade Mark and me for the Director or they will kill her."

Jack's eyes turned icy green. He said, "Why don't we pray and ask the Father what to do before we do what I feel like doing?"

Everyone was starting to kneel when Raquel appeared in his Archangel form. "Jack, I have a word from the Most High for you." *"My child, as usual, the demonic is attempting to cloud the issues. Again, they are inserting demons without permission in an attempt to destroy the entire Crossfire Team, especially Mark and Christi. Know this; they will not let Director Jakobson live unless you take her from them. Be aware that Satan did not do this himself. I can now tell you a dark secret from before the time of the Garden of Eden. Satan and the dark Angels fell to the Earth at the dawn of mankind. A covenant I made with Satan included the wording that I would not reveal this secret unless it was used to contravene my authority. In the desire to rid the Earth of the Crossfire Team and others this secret has been used to contravene my authority. Therefore, I am now released from this covenant that I made thousands of years ago. Satan is not omnipotent nor is he omnipresent. He complained that he could not control his demonic kingdom on such a grand scale without those attributes. I would not give him that. To offset that argument, I agreed that he could rise up six helpers, as capable as he, and he could place one of them on the Earth forever. This being is equal in all things except ultimate authority to Satan. I have been unable to tell you this because of the covenant of old. Now, I can tell you that you have been fighting this old Earth Demon, not Satan himself. This is one reason that Satan has been so outraged by my use of your team in his domain. He hasn't been the one attacking your team; it has been his Earth Demon. He is the one that has been using the demons to attack humankind directly. He is also the one that has determined the Crossfire Team must be destroyed. He is also the one that has imitated Satan in combat with you in the Human Dimension. I could not guide you to attack this Earth Demon without violating the covenant. That time is now past. This demon has presented himself as a disguised human so long he thinks he is a human. He controls many humans and demons, but, he is a truly a demon. He has had many names since he became Satan on Earth. His present name is Zagon; He has residences in several different countries. He is in his North American residence while he focuses the attempts to destroy your team. He has violated the covenant by not being obedient to my authority, by attempting to destroy what is mine, and doing what I have expressly told his master Satan not to do. Zagon has done a great deal of this without Satan's knowledge. Therefore, I command you to take My Holy Anger to him. I will let you pursue him until he realizes, he cannot escape, cannot hide, and he cannot beat you. Show him no mercy. I will tell Satan after you destroy Zagon that next time he allows this form of defiance; I will not restrain you and your forces from destroying Satan himself. He will finally realize that I AM God and I will change history, scripture, and prophesy to destroy him. Do it now. I will be with you as will My Holy warriors."*

The fire in Raquel's eyes matched the icy coldness in Jack's. Raquel nodded to Jack and disappeared. Jack keyed the All Personnel switch and called a full team meeting in the Living Area in fifteen minutes.

Everybody was early to the meeting. Jack stood up and had everyone else sit down. "Well, people, this is a big one. A new devil, named Zagon who has ruled Earth in secret for Satan, has kidnapped the Director of the Mossad, Iris Jakobson. He wants to swap her for Mark and Christi. I say no, the Father says no with prejudice. The Father has commanded us to go on the offensive and to destroy this earthbound demon and, if necessary, we will go to the demonic dimension as much as we have to until we have rescued the Mossad Director and driven the devil to his knees, then we are to take him out. God says that he is an equal in power to Satan but works for him. Zagonhas defied Heaven one too many times in his own power without approval even from Satan."

"When we take him out, God is willing to rewrite history, scripture, and prophesy, if Satan doesn't obey Heaven's orders in the future. We have been given the privilege to go find Zagon, rescue Iris and totally destroy that particular evil. We are going to start in about one hour. There may be rest breaks and possibly even time to sleep. But, I think they will be rare and I will tell you now, you are going to be filled with a Holy Anger against Satan and his followers. We will take out all demons and anything demonic any way we can. Sergeant Howell, is there any of that special ammo that Mark's Team used on the road trip to hell still available?"

Sgt. Howell stood up. "General, I checked that vault last week and there were only a couple of hundred rounds left. I checked that tonight and the entire vault is crammed with the ammo, missiles, grenades, and 40mm rifle grenades."

Mark commented, "God doesn't miss any details, does He?"

Jack nodded, "Distribute a full load to every man and woman and arrange for transport of as much as possible with us wherever we go. Elon! I'm going to appoint you as our interface with the Mossad. You keep them up to date with what we are doing. It's their Director and I know they want in on this as much or even more than we do. But, tell them where we're going they can't go. Not without dying. Also, tell them that we will get the job done for them."

Jack told everyone to get ready to go. Now, he had to find out where they were going. He spoke very loudly into the air."Raquel!"

Raquel appeared next to Jack. "The demons still have Director Jakobson here on Earth. Actually they are still in Israel. You know it's definitely a trap for you, Mark, and Christi, right?"

Jack nodded, "Where are they located and what can we do to prevent them from transitioning back into the demonic realm when they realize the trap has backfired and they are losing?"

Raquel smiled, "We will prevent them from escaping and from killing the Director if we have to. Your Team can handle the demons. I will have another destination for you when you're done with these creatures." A map appeared floating in the air in front of Jack and Mark. Raquel pointed to the location where they were holding the Mossad Director. "It's an old Mansion that was converted to a business over a hundred years ago."

Raquel faded out and Jack asked Ethan, "Did you get the map?"Ethan nodded, "Yeah, and I got a floor plan and a new x-ray view of the place off of a LandSat bird." He made a couple of entries. "Okay, all of that is in your battle/COMMs."

Jack looked around and spotted Christi taking notes. "Christi, I want you to hang with Laura and Alexis for this campaign because I think they want you more than anyone else except Mark."

He motioned for Laura and Alexis to come up to the front. When they were there Jack told them, "Be on alert for attempted demonic snatch and grab operations for Christi. You guys will be probably more the point of the spear than anyone else with the exception of Mark. If things get out of hand, let me know. You two good?"

Both women nodded, took Christi in tow and headed for the Armory.

CHAPTER SEVENTEEN

Jack motioned to Su Li and Mark White. "You two are going to be busy. Mike, I want you to handle logistics for two R&D "Ghosts", especially maintenance and damage repair as well as fuel and ammo supply. Use my name and rank with the Mossad and the IAF (Israeli Air Force) to have fuel, or repair teams anywhere we have to go. Be ready to switch vehicles at a moment's notice."

He looked at Su Li. "Su Li, I want you to handle team/target operations with the aircraft. You both are trained sword bearers. Defend the aircraft any way you have to. We will be using the FGs with both aircraft so hopefully you won't have to defend them. You both are very smart and inventive, use that."

Jack looked at the warriors and saw that they were ready. "All right people, we've got a Director to save and a devil to hunt down, let's do it!"

Jack prayed for a reappearance of Raquel. The Angel Caleb showed up instead. "Hello Jack, Raquel is not available right now, he sent me, and how can I help you?"

Jack smiled at the angel. "Hello Caleb, my old friend, the question is; if we corner Zagon won't he just flee to Heaven and plead for God to save him from us?"

Caleb shook his head. "Until he is destroyed, Heaven is closed to him. The Most High has determined that this action will resolve Zagon's disobedience. If Satan continues to use these tactics to elevate his place above that of God, he will not be able to escape your Team either. I will tell you that this is the first time in known history that a cleansing at this level has happened. Good hunting." Caleb faded out of sight and Jack ran into the Armory.

As Jack loaded up with the special ammunition and other weapons, he wasn't surprised to find another one of the spears with the tip of crystal. He knew who that spear was for. In his earpiece he heard Su Li quietly tell him that the Ghosts were warmed up and ready on the tarmac outside of the Crossfire Team Base Entry."

Jack acknowledged her call and whistled loudly. He waved everyone out of the Armory and to the air strip.

He held the spear in his right hand and felt the perfect balance. The tip gleamed brightly and the spear vibrated in his hand. Then the spear disappeared. Jack knew it would be ready when it was needed.

Before he left he opened the vault located in the Armory and took two of the older belt style FGs with him.

He ran to the second Ghost and handed one FG to Mark. "Fix this on the frame and turn it on." He ran to the first Ghost and climbed on board. He mounted and activated the FG and felt the tingle that told him it was working. The LED showed green. He keyed his mic on his battle/COMM and told the pilots to move out.

He switched the FG hooked to the Ghost to "special" just before they exited the flight corridor and came out from under the island off the Israeli coast. They made a bee-line to their target and reached the place in less than ten minutes. Jack had everyone set the switch on their Body Armor to the "special" setting for their FGs. Everyone faded out of sight.

Su Li and Mike White set the two Ghosts down just outside the mansion. It still impressed him somewhat when he looked over to where the second Ghost was and he could not see it.

The troops exited the aircraft and formed up as Mark told them to do. "Remember; don't use the new ammo and explosives until I tell you to. We need to keep that a secret until when we have Iris safely in our hands.

The first barrier was a massive gate that had protected the Mansion for over 150 years. One 40mm rifle grenade knocked the gate from the wall and the troops flowed into the grounds, surrounding the house.

Christi listened to Alexis as she moved with her and Laura. Then she started praying. Her armor and sword appeared and she went to the high guard position with her sword over her right shoulder. Laura and Alexis matched the younger woman as they went up the six steps to the side door to the living quarters of the Mansion. It was a vision of anger, violence, and faith that no one could see coming.

Suddenly, all three Force Generators shut down and everyone became visible and much more vulnerable. Christi shook her head and turned to her left and used her right foot to kick open the twelve-foot high door right at the latch. As they moved forward into the building, two dozen demons came at them.

All three women engaged the demons and battled for their lives. Laura went into time management technique and eliminated two of the demons in one pass. Alexis was weaving in and out around three more of the more human demons and used her sword to cripple and then kill all three.

Christi used everything she had been given on sword combat but couldn't break through the defensive swordplay of the sleek demon she was fighting. She tried several feints and follow-throughs but the enemy seemed to know the defenses for these actions. Christi attempted to disengage to rethink her attack but the demon pressed her and started to use new things that Christi had not learned yet. Christi was forced backward and was totally defensive.

A bright blade cut through the demon's neck, ending the attack on her. As the demon's body dropped to the floor, Christi looked at Alexis standing in front of her and nodded her thanks. Then they both went back to the battle. No more had Christi engaged another demon than something hit her on her left side very hard. Her armor prevented any penetration and blunted the attack, but the impact of the large black blade almost knocked the air out of Christi's lungs.

Christi stepped forward rather than back up and that saved her from more slamming as the demon ran into Laura and lost his arm and his sword. These items were quickly followed by his head. Christi went to high guard and looked around but, she didn't find any more demons.

Laura came over and had Christi stop praying for a few seconds while she checked for broken ribs or anything like that. "Well, young lady, you're going to have some colorful bruises but nothing severe."

Christi started praying again and her armor and sword reappeared. She sucked in a deep breath, "Ohh! That smarts." Laura smiled and nodded her head.

Laura called Jack on her battle/COMM. "Jack, what happened to our FGs?"

Jack came back breathing hard, "I don't know as yet but I suspect the demonic has found a way to make the FGs think the operate switch is turned off. We've got eyes on the Director and she is still alive. All three of you head for the front hall and entry where we are."

Nine demons later the three women reached the front hall and joined in the melee ensuing there. Christi saw the older woman held by one demon that held a sword to her throat. Alexis was cutting down demons and dodging black blades and a persistent little demon with four eyes and six legs. She couldn't take time to kill it without giving a big opening to the larger demons that were also attacking her.

Mark spoke over the battle/COMM. On the count of three, everyone who can break off, do that, stop praying and use your handgun or rifle. I will take care of the Director. Three, two, one, Now!"

Golden and silver armor disappeared all over the scene of the battle and handguns and several rifles began to spit the special ammo with loud reports. The small, crystal nose on the bullets was flowing with the Esteem of Yahveh and each one killed a demon. Christi shot the little demon at Alexis' feet and it turned into smoke and stain.

Mark had drawn his .40 caliber XD autoloader and carefully shot the demon holding Iris in its head. The demon died and his sword disappeared before he could cut the Director's throat. She staggered away from the dying demon and found Jack on one side of her and Mark on the other.

In less than thirty seconds the building was empty of demons and everyone took a knee or sat down and rested while they had time. Each person thanked God the Father and Yahshua for their success and survival. For a person who fought real, physical demons, it was very clear that God was the force or power that allowed the person to prevail.

David Zahavy came into the hall and went over to Mark. He quietly whispered into Mark's ear. Mark stepped back and looked at David with a frown. "You're sure?" David nodded his head. Mark and David walked over to where Jack and Laura were praying off the curses and assignments the demons had infested the Director with while they had control over her.

When Jack was sure God had cleansed the Director of anything the demons had cursed her with, he looked up at Mark, "You don't look happy. What's the problem?"

CHAPTER EIGHTEEN

Mark included the Director as a part of the discussion. "Madam Director, I am sorry to have to tell you this, but there is a complete, five-person Kidon squad in a room on the second floor and they are all dead. It looks like they entered the room during the battle. They expended a lot of rounds but did not hurt the demon or demons they found there. The evidence indicates that they were either bludgeoned or stabbed to death. Before we came here, I had Elon advise them not to attempt to be part of our battles because they are not anointed by God nor are they equipped to do so."

Jack took Iris' hand, "I am also sad that the Kidon team was killed. Can you convince them to stop offering their lives when they have no chance to win?"

Iris looked at Jack. "Could they have won and still be alive if you had given them some of that awesome ammunition you mentioned?"

Jack knew the answer but instead spoke into the air, "Raquel?"

The Arch Angel appeared in his fierce armor with demon stain running off of it. He looked at Jack but spoke to Iris. "The reason Jack could not share the ammunition with the members of the Kidon squad is because the essence of Yahveh is part of each munition and cannot be handled by someone who is not anointed and cleansed by Yahveh because their sin burden causes them to be affected just like a demon. They might not die but they would be so adversely affected by the essence of Yahveh that they would not survive combat. Each person must be completely committed to God's Son to use that ammunition. I and those with me tried to save them but there were too many of the enemy, I am sorry."

Iris nodded her head and asked if she could address the rest of the Crossfire Team. Jack used his battle/COM to get quiet and order. He gave Iris a wireless microphone that linked her into the battle/COM he was using.

Iris wiped the tears from her eyes. "Members of the Crossfire Team. I want to thank each and every one of you that offered up their lives to rescue me from that spiritual filth. I will see that Israel recognizes you for your services to the Nation of Israel. Keep up the good work."

She handed the microphone back to Jack. She turned to Mark and David, "Show me, please."

As the three of them walked off to the stairs, Charlie Wu and Ethan Reaper approached Jack. Charlie nodded to Jack. "We've been in contact with Dr. Clashire and he agrees that the demonic switched off our FGs. But, they did it spiritually, not physically. That is why turning the FGs off and back on did not work. We have prayed and the Father told us to tell you to gather all of the Team together." Charlie swept the scope of the room with his left arm, "They are all here except for Mark and David."

About then the two men in question entered the room and walked over to Jack.

Raquel appeared and asked everyone to make sure their FG was in the "off" position. Then he rose to a height of about ten feet. He held out his hands. Rays of golden light speared out of his hands to each of the FGs in the body armor for a few seconds. Then the rays disappeared and Raquel announced, "Your FGs will function correctly from now on, regardless what the demons do".

Raquel dropped down to the floor level and quietly explained the problem. "Satan's demons were given information from a source I am looking to reveal. He was able to use a basic sixth Dimension power to set the Force Generators to the "off" setting. What the Most High had me do was to shield the Force Generators against any attempt to spiritually change any physical conditions of the Generators, especially the control circuitry. How did your Team manage during the loss of the Force Generators?"

Jack shrugged his shoulders, "We have two wounded badly enough that I put them on the injured list and they get to stay at the base until they're healed. Christi was banged pretty hard but, she has opted to stay with the field Team. She's going to have some major bruises and pain, but nothing is broken."

Raquel spotted Christi leaning against the wall and holding her side under her body armor. He went over to her and smiled at her. She smiled weakly back at the handsome Archangel. Raquel took her hand away from her injured rib cage and put his hand there. He looked deeply into her eyes and saw the spark of healing surge through her. His plea to the Most High had been answered. He removed his hand and walked back to Jack and Mark. "Never underestimate a demonic wound, even through your spiritual armor. They had implanted an extremely dangerous spiritual wound that would have killed her if it had not been healed by the Most High." He looked at Jack, "You healed one just like this when you prayed for Alexis about a month ago."

Jack recalled putting his hand on Alexis and God healing her, but, he didn't realize the depth of the wound. He prayed silently, "Thank you Father, for healing Alexis through my prayers, even though I didn't know she had been spiritually injured. I confess my ignorance as sin and repent of it. Forgive me my sins Father and let me walk in your light. Amen." He said to Raquel, "I will have to pray for the two injured men." Raquel shook his head. "Your mission is too important for that. I will see to it for you."

Jack squeezed the switch on his body armor and was greatly relieved when he saw the LED turn green again. He got on his knees and prayed to God for the strategy for his next move against Zagon.

Jack was resting in the Lord when he got a name. Nothing more, just a name, "Raquel".

Jack got up and spoke into the air, "Raquel?"

Raquel appeared in his body armor version. He sat down with Jack at a table in the hall. "Jack, your next step is to go after the devil. I can translate your entire Team into the demonic realm, if need be, so that you can fight your way to him. Since you have been faithful to ask, I will fill all of your warriors with the Most High's Holy Anger and instill a desire to fulfill God's wishes."

Jack agreed and immediately felt the power and the urge that he had felt before when he had been filled with God's Holy Anger.

Jack had all the troops gather around and had them switch on their Force Generators. He reassigned the sub teams and Mark got them organized. The twelve people in the Core Team each had three people with them. Christi was assigned to Laura and Alexis again.

Over the next ten hours they eliminated hundreds of demons of all kinds. Jack saw increasingly higher level demons leading the defenses. Eventually they reached the level of demons that a single warrior could not defeat the leader by themselves. Still, most of these fled the field of battle.

Jack called Raquel and asked for a break for the troops. Raquel gave them a complete rest break which lasted for about ten hours and allowed the Team to rest, eat, clean up and pray. When they resumed their war, only ten seconds had elapsed on their combat clock.

CHAPTER NINETEEN

As they were getting ready to return to combat, Christi cornered Jack. "Tell me about our target, excuse me, Zagon."

Jack grinned, "Zagon is our target. Well, you know about PRDS, correct?"

Christi looked thoughtful but shook her head. "I have heard the term but I don't know what that means."

Jack nodded; PRDS is a short form of PaRDeS which refers to types of approaches to biblical interpretation of text in Torah study. PaRDeS is an acronym formed from the name initials of the following four approaches:"

"Peshat; This is the plain or simple or direct meaning. In other words, Peshat means that what you think of when you read a Scripture and it says something like, "The lamb walks a dangerous path." The Peshat of this statement means that a soft fluffy animal goes down a path that has peril or danger for it."

"Remez; This study is of the "hints" or the deep (hidden or symbolic) meaning beyond just the literal sense. This level of study would say that the statement, "The lamb walks a dangerous path." Actually means that the Lamb of God (Yahshua/Jesus) is charting a perilous course of life."

"Derash; which means to "inquire" or "seek" as in the Midrashic meaning as given through similar occurrences. This is where you get Heavenly revelation by connecting the dots. You begin to see where this Scripture has deep meaning connected to other Scriptures."

"Sod; Means "Secret" or Mystery which means as given through inspiration or revelation. When you read a Scripture you seek God for the mystery represented by this particular text. Everything the Hebrew studies has a physical and a spiritual meaning."

"Each type of Pardes interpretation examines the extended meaning of a Scripture. As a general rule, the extended meaning never contradicts the base meaning. The Peshat means the plain or contextual meaning of the text. Remez is the allegorical meaning. Derash includes the metaphorical meaning, and Sod represents the hidden meaning. There is often considerable overlap."

Jack smiled at the young woman. "You are probably wondering why I am telling you about Pardes. Because I want you to understand there are mysteries and hidden meanings and things in Scripture and in the supernatural world. Zagon is an Earthly equivalent of Satan. It has all the powers and evil of the original but is bound to the Earth and cannot transition between dimensions like Satan can. It works for Satan and has been on the Earth before mankind appeared after Yahveh created them."

"Zagon runs the demonic world on Earth but, he still is subservient to Satan. Satan is not like God, he isn't omnipotent, nor is he omnipresent. He can't see all things and be all places, especially at one time. So, God allowed Satan to create six beings just like himself but controlled by him."

"Zagon is the root cause of all our problems on this Earth. You've never heard of him because there was a binding covenant between Yahveh God and Satan around the time of the Garden of Eden. One stipulation in that covenant was that God would not reveal the presence of Zagon unless he did anything that went against the express will of God. It turns out that it was Zagon rather than Satan that has been bringing demons with physical bodies into the human dimension and Zagon is the one that we have run head-long into that has resulted in this war we're in at the moment."

"The interesting thing about this is that some spiritually aware people know about Satan and his evil ways and his demons. Everyone talks about Satan as the most wanted devil. But nobody talks about Zagon because he was hidden for all history until now. I think this is God's way of getting rid of a hidden sore spot quietly. While Satan gets the spotlight and ends up in the Lake of Fire. In truth, Zagon will also end up there regardless when he dies physically."

Christi nodded her head. "I see what you mean about hidden things in the supernatural. I wonder if I study my whole life if I can even scratch the surface of the supernatural world."

Jack chuckled, "You don't have to worry about that. In thirty-seven months you are going to be drawn up to Heaven by Yahshua for the rest of eternity and nothing that you didn't get to do will ever bother you again."

Christi laughed, "I hope I get my mission accomplished by then."

Jack stood up when Christi did and gave her a hug, "Don't worry, Yahveh doesn't make mistakes and He said you would finish your mission."

Christi just nodded her head.

Jack walked over to Mark who was talking to Raquel. Jack looked at Raquel. When Mark saw him he stopped their conversation. Jack asked the Archangel, "What is our next target and where has Zagon gone to now?"

Raquel stared at Jack for several seconds. "Zagon is moving right now. He is headed for an Egyptian operational center. I believe he is going to stop relying on demons to defend him since they can't defeat you. He will call in many human troops to defend him. You know he doesn't care if you killed the whole human race as long as they could protect him. They mean nothing to him other than what they can do for him."

Mark looked at Jack. "It looks like it is time for a small party that is really stealthy and we go for Zagon himself rather than chewing up people and demons to get at him."

Jack nodded, "Okay, four people and one Archangel. That will be you, me, Alexis, Christi, and Raquel."

Raquel nodded his head. Mark asked, "Why that group?"

Jack shrugged his shoulders, "I have the spear, you are our best warrior, Christi because the Father says to take her with us on all missions, and Alexis because she and Christi have seemed to have bonded during combat."

Jack thought for a second, "I want the rest of the Team just out of detection range with Sarah, David, and Laura, each in charge of a third of the Team."

Mark nodded and left to organize the teams.

Raquel had remained quiet but now he questioned the splitting up of the Team with Christi in the most perilous group. "Are we endangering Christi and her mission by putting her in such an "active" position?"

Jack looked at the Archangel. "I would think that if anyone would know the answer to that, it would be you."

Raquel smiled, "Thank you for your insight Jack Malone. Yes, I would be the most informed but one of my tasks is to see if you question yourself as to your decisions. I see that you think things out before you announce actions. That is a good sign. And No, I am given whatever I know by the Most High and he seems to be agreeing with you. So, let us be about our business."

"Show us the location of the Egyptian operation and any traps you know about." Jack had already decided what they were going to do and now he just needed as much information as possible.

CHAPTER TWENTY

Jack realized that he had selected the Ghosts because he had been led to do that by the Father. They were already in the Jordanian Desert where they had just defeated Zagon's most massively defended hard site.

Jack installed the older FG that Raquel had "fixed" so that the enemy couldn't control it remotely. He set the switch to "Special" and the Ghost emulated its name and disappeared to outside view. Su Li and Mike White had learned to depend on detecting each other's ID chip to position their aircraft while in flight during invisibility. Since the Ghosts were autonomous they knew where the other plane was through some means of their own. As the two Ghosts flew to the Egyptian site Jack called the attack team together.

"All right folks, "Jack said, "I really want this to be the finale for the Zagon operation. Raquel, I need you to positively identify Zagon as the target when we are approaching. I'm sure he has at least one duplicate to use as a red herring." Seeing the curious look on the Angel's face, he explained, "A red herring means a false lead that looks real but in truth, is not." Raquel nodded.

Jack continued, "I want you three to defend me as I give Zagon his present. I'm sure he will get the point. Let's stay invisible until the last second. That may make the job easier. We'll see."

The Ghost set down on the ground several hundred feet away from the building which was half buried in the sand. The five members of the attack team got up and left the vehicle, they were followed by all the other members.

Jack spoke quietly. "According to the plans that Ethan got for us, there are six rooms on the first floor and five on the second. But, there are a series of rooms underneath the house according to the LandSat scans. These are rooms that don't show on the plans for the building. I would expect that Zagon is down there since demonic beings prefer caves or other underground dwellings."

Raquel frowned, "Do you really think that a being with the power of Satan would be hiding in the lower area rather than being on top?"

Jack smiled, "He is being hunted by a force that is unstoppable and implacable. That could make him run to a place of security in his eyes. Jack thought some more. "Plus I would guess that since Zagon has been doing this without Satan's permission and it is now causing great trouble for Satan, he may not be getting support from below."

By then they had reached the massive stone building, supposedly built in that fashion to repel the heat of the desert but in reality, it was a stone fortress. Jack said, "Go to the right and we should find a down ramp to an entrance to the lower level."

The four people and the Angel found the ramp and eventually a door. Raquel mentioned, "This is where the security forces would lay the best traps and defenses."

Jack had been praying and felt a definite leading to go to this door. "Let's see what we can do.

Mark's voice came over the battle/COMM, "In for a dime, in for a dollar."

Raquel asked what currency had to do with this situation. Mark told him it was just a saying that if you are going to do a small bit you might as well go for it all.

Christi listened to the men and angel talk and she walked up and turned the door handle. Everyone held their breath as the door swung open. Nothing happened and there didn't seem to be any alarm.

Jack said, "Fall back now!" Everyone went to the top end of the ramp. Nothing happened for the next few minutes. Alexis snorted, "There is no way a major entry to the hiding place of a Satan wanta-be who is worried for his safety would be unlocked, unguarded, and not alarmed. Something is just not right."

Suddenly there was such a bright light no one could see. The light died down after a few seconds and it was obvious what the devil had done.

Mark said, "O'yeah, it was wired, it was a trigger for a field-grade tactical nuclear weapon."

Jack looked around and there was nothing standing for thousands of feet in any direction. Where the house stood was a huge crater still glowing from the explosion.

Christi shook her head, which no one could see, "I can't believe any being is so evil it would kill all the people around here just to kill us. I am really mad now."

Raquel mentioned that the rest of the team and the aircraft were intact and unhurt.

Jack looked over and could see the place where the aircraft had been sitting with the reserve troops gathered around it, although nothing was visible.

Jack stood there for several minutes. "Okay, Raquel, I want you to find this demon and let's stop him once and forever."

CHAPTER TWENTY-ONE

Raquel told Jack he would return and faded away. Jack told everyone to stay in their "special" settings and leave the Ghost that way also. He ordered the reserve team to board the Ghost. The four Team members made their way back to the Ghost and entered. Jack set his FG back to "normal" and everyone else followed suit. Jack told the Ghost to slowly go up to twenty thousand feet and cruise toward Israel.

Ethan and Charlie called Jack over to where they were seated. Charlie tipped his head toward Ethan. "This is one very inventive guy. He had an idea that could help us. He figured out how to lock onto a Crossfire Medallion and show its location. The person wearing the Medallion is indicated. It doesn't work at any substantial distance but it is a great help for anyone working with another cloaked person or even a ship. Or, in this case when you are working with three other, invisible, people. I doubt that anyone else has a Medallion that would have the unique ID properties of our Medallions."

Jack asked Ethan "How long will it take to install it on all of our communications equipment to give each of us a physical location of other Medallions in their eyepieces.

Ethan smiled, "About thirty seconds, want to try it?"

Jack nodded his head. Ethan built a small program in about twelve seconds and then propagated it to all the other people's communications systems.

Jack stood up and Ethan said, "Just say the password, "Coin Hunt". Jack did so and suddenly he had a graphic he could see in his combat eyepiece that showed a set of initials with a circle around them for each person on the aircraft. Surrounding all of them was a big circle with the initials AC at the top. Jack asked Ethan, what is the big circle with the initials AC?"

Ethan smiled, "That would be the Ghost. The AC means Air Craft."

Jack smiled, "This is great Ethan. Congratulations and thanks from all of us. Now, explain it to Mark and the other people on the other Ghost, please."

Ethan presented the new capability to everyone else in the group. He got them all to experiment with it. "There could be unknowns that haven't cropped up as yet. If you experience anything new or unusual, let me know. Thanks." He got a standing ovation from the Team. Mark came over and slapped Ethan on the back in happiness. "Now I don't have to wonder who's with me and where they are, and they will know where to go. I owe you a steak dinner young man."

Ethan finished coughing from Mark's slap to his back and then he laughed, "You ain't seen anything yet and I will take you up on that steak dinner."

Raquel appeared next to Jack. "I have a definite destination where we will find Zagon. It is in the United States and it is in Washington, D.C. not too far from the Capitol Building. I believe he knows how much trouble your team is in with the U.S. authorities and he probably feels that you would not come after him there."

Jack felt the Holy Anger building in him. "They don't matter right now. Neither they, nor he will see us coming. This time, we are a force of God that can't be stopped!"

Jack told the Ghost to use the low heat protocol and put them down as close to the location that Raquel gave the plane as possible.

Two hours later both Ghosts had taken on a fresh load of fuel from an Israeli Tanker and flew to the U.S. They silently grounded less than a block away from the target building. Raquel left the craft and returned almost immediately. "Zagon is in the building in the largest room and it is him, definitely. He has over three hundred human soldiers around the house, in the house, even forty of them in the room he is in. He also has three legions of demons ranked around the residence and in the room he is in. He has several escape routes and a bullet-proof cage around him. One of the escape routes is straight down at the instant anything is detected."

Jack asked Raquel, "Can you block that?"

Raquel smiled, "Absolutely."

Jack said, "Same teams, let's do it."

The four humans and the Archangel walked up to the front entrance and waited for the door to open. One of the human henchmen walked out to have a cigarette. While he was exiting, the invisible team slipped into the foyer which was easy because the front doors were electric and both opened at once.

Following Raquel, they avoided the hard men and waited for someone to use the elevator to the lower floor. A man who was so ugly he could have been a demon entered the elevator and the others crammed in behind him. While it was true the rider could not have missed the additional company it didn't matter since he died standing there. To him it felt like he had a carbon arc flame applied to his brain. The combat knife in his kidney was so painful he could not even scream. Mark held the dead man in an upright position as the doors opened on the major floor in the lower level. The man whose job it was to watch the people that came down in the elevator knew immediately that there was something wrong but he didn't raise an alarm because the last man that did that was flayed alive in front of everybody for raising a false alarm.

Before he could conclude that this was a real problem he also died on his feet without a sound.

Jack and Christi casually stepped around the guard and walked over and peered into the bullet-proof glass cage in the middle of the room. Zagon was sitting in a throne-like chair talking on the phone.

The Holy Anger in Jack was building and he wasted no time on showmanship. He held his right hand down and felt the weight of the spear fill his hand. He stepped forward and hurled the spear at the demon with all the force he had. The spear, with the Esteem of Yahveh rolling off of the crystal point in waves, penetrated the glass cage with the bullet-proof glass as if it wasn't even there.

Zagon discerned the threat and pushed the button to drop the chair and him to freedom. Nothing happened. He saw the spear coming and he placed an impenetrable force field between the spear and himself.

Mark watched as the spear ignored the force field and slammed into the ages old demon. The horrid scream he emitted as he was consumed by the Holy Fire of God was a poor second to the one Moloch had screamed when Mark had terminated him in the demonic dimension several months ago. Jack used his battle/COMM, "All Team Members switch to "normal" on your Force Generators. All teams attack now!"

The sudden appearance of four armed humans in the main room caused a great upheaval as they began to cut down everyone in the place. Rifles and handguns were drawn by the humans and they shot at all the gold and silver armored warriors with hundreds of rounds without effect. The legions of demons saw Raquel and raced to return to the demonic dimension. Some thousands of them never made it because suddenly it seemed the entire Host of Heaven appeared and set upon the demons. With the Host ahead of them and Raquel behind them they scattered and most of them died in the process.

Christi was not familiar with the heady power of the Wrath of God and His Holy Anger. She set to destroying anyone and everyone she could reach. Ten more of the Team came through the front doors and joined the attack on everyone there.

To Jack it seemed when he came up against the henchmen of Zagon that he had a flash of the evil each one had committed on the Earth in his mind. Their callous evils of torture and murder of the innocent and each outrage just added to the anger filling him. He realized that God was giving him a one-second court trial of each person and the verdict condemning that person to hell. He noticed that it was a trial in front of God and nothing was hidden or forgotten. Their destruction was assured and ordered by God.

Once finished with their work there they made their way upstairs and joined in the destruction on the higher level. For the first time all the evil doers and hard men met God's messengers and people more powerful and stronger than them. They died screaming like the poor souls they had slaughtered before.

An hour later, there were no more enemy to be eliminated. Jack called all the troops together and kneeled in the blood and bodies and prayed for God's peace which came in abundance. Then they stood and walked to the doors in the front of the building. Outside there were over one hundred law enforcement and Military personnel with their weapons all pointed at the Team.

Jack walked out in front of the Team. "Whoever is in charge here needs to go into this building and see who perished in here. God commanded that these animals be destroyed to keep them from preying on you and your citizens. They will not be bothering you again, ever."

The U.S. Army One Star General, Myron Ross stepped forward. "Regardless of your supposed justification, you and your troops have committed murder here on a grand scale and you will be arrested and held until you have been tried before a court of law in this land. Our troops outnumber you three to one and we are arresting you in the name of the law."

Jack was praying to Yahveh. He clearly heard, *"You walk in My righteousness and as I said, I will never desert you nor forsake you. Behold your troops."*

Jack looked back and lost his breath. Visible behind the Team, in the air, were thousands of armed Angels and Archangels ranked in formation above the house behind him. The Glory of God shown around all of the Angels and also the Crossfire Team.

God spoke in a voice of such power the elements shook. ***"These are My warriors! And they are doing as I have commanded! I told your Senators, and now I will tell you. Any of you that bless these warriors I will bless, any of you that curse these warriors I will curse. Be warned, this day I call the heavens and the earth as witnesses against you that I have set before you life and death, blessings and curses. Now choose life, so that you and your children may live."***

A great silence fell over the entire area. It seemed that all creation stood still and listened to the Creator of the Universe. The soldiers and police lowered their weapons. Jack spoke on his battle/COMM. "Follow me to the Ghost, keep your heads up and walk in quietness and confidence."

He turned and walked past the General and the soldiers and the law enforcement personnel, the Team followed him as he used Ethan's new software to locate the hidden aircraft. They reached the invisible Ghost and Jack ushered all of the Team into the Jet and then climbed onboard himself. He told the two Ghosts to return to the

Sea Base and to leave with maximum power and flair. He switched the FG hooked to the plane to "normal" as David Zahavy did the same on the second Ghost.

The two futuristic aircraft suddenly appeared before the U.S. Army troops and the combined law enforcement personnel. Both aircraft rose from the ground into the air and smoothly tipped back until their noses were pointed straight up. Then they shook the whole area with a massive roar as they climbed straight up on two pillars of fire each.

Eight anti-aircraft missiles flew from multiple points at the aircraft. One angel held his sword point toward the aircraft and all eight missiles exploded at once and rained fragments and flaming debris everywhere including on the assembled police and military units.

Completely ignoring the attacks, the Ghosts quickly built speed until they disappeared into the clouds at a phenomenal rate.

The Angels broke ranks, turned individually and seemed to walk into the distance, disappearing as they went. It was beyond humbling for the humans watching.

As the rumble of the mysterious aircraft faded away in the distance, the senior law enforcement officer told the Army General, "General Ross, I don't know why the government keeps ticking these people off. They are obviously fighting for us and in case you didn't notice, they have us way outgunned."

The General sighed, "I know and I got the very clear message from God. I don't know about you, Phil, but I'm submitting my resignation today. Right after I submit my recommendation supporting the efforts by the Crossfire Team and what they did here today. Regardless of what the One-World-Government wants, I am not going to fight against God and Heaven."

Phil looked at the senior Military man and asked, "How do you know that was really God and those were really angels?"

Myron Ross looked deeply into his friend's eyes. "Phil, you obviously don't know how to identify God's voice. I do, and I assure you that was Him. You need to go home, get on your knees and pray that God will speak to you so you know the truth. Otherwise you are going to go to an eternal barbeque with you as the main entrée."

Phil knew the General very well. He knew when he was speaking the unvarnished truth, like right now.

CHAPTER TWENTY-TWO

Everyone more or less collapsed into their seats after securing their weapons and equipment in the storage area in the back of the plane. Jack felt the bone weary tiredness and agreed that they all needed to rest. Mark was sitting next to Jack and muttered. "There are always pluses and minuses to everything aren't there? I mean, we get to use the "Ghost", the "Myth", and the "Figment" that travel so fast it takes almost no time between continents. That's a huge plus. The negative is that there is not time to really get any rest between points. When we're tired that's a negative we need to take into our planning."

Jack looked at his watch, "Yeah, well, you just wasted two percent of your rest during this flight time telling me that."

Mark shook his head, "Aahh, the miracles of modern air travel."

Jack told the Ghost to make it dark in the passenger compartment before he realized that there was no other compartment on the aircraft. There was a low level glow to the view screens representing windows that kept the interior from being claustrophobic. Jack was glad that the designers had thought of that detail. Then, suddenly he woke up as the aircraft sounded a hushed alert sound as it lowered its wheels for landing at the Sea Base.

CHAPTER TWENTY-THREE

As the Ghosts had approached the Israeli Coast, Jack and David had switched the FG on each of their aircraft back to "special" and the planes again disappeared from sight. After they were in the tunnel flyway to the actual base, they switched back to "normal" and then shut them off and removed them. After returning the planes to the R&D group, the entire Crossfire Team carried their equipment into their base. They all went through the cleaning of their equipment, turning it in to the Armory, and doing their After-Action reports.

The SOG Sergeant who kept the audit on equipment at the armory quietly told Jack that the special vault they kept the special ammo and weapons was completely full again.

Jack released everyone until the next morning at 9:00 A.M. when he wanted to hold a prayer session for the entire team at the Synagogue for the great effort that they had accomplished.

Sarah looked tiredly at her husband as they made their way to their apartment. "Well, husband dear, it seems like you didn't face down Satan but Zagon instead."

Mark smiled, "You underestimate me again dear wife, and I faced down the one and only Satan twice."

Sarah shook her head, "Didn't you hear God say that all our combat has been against Zagon instead of Satan?"

Mark nodded as he let them both into their apartment. "I also remember that either God or Raquel; I can't remember which, told us that Zagon never left Earth since the days of Adam and Eve. I believe my two encounters with his evilness were in the Demonic Dimension. That would be the real Satan, not the late and not-so-great Zagon."

Sarah thought back. "Ohh, yeah. Well, you know that means the real Satan still hates your guts and wants to fillet you over a slow fire."

Mark laughed, "Let him try."

A half-hour later, the base was as quiet as it had been before everyone got back.

The next morning after the prayer session in the Crossfire Synagogue, the Team got back to a more-or-less routine for several days.

Two days after their return, the Core Team had a short meeting to get closure for what Mark called the "Demonic Onslaught Era". They discussed all the actions since Zagon, a demon, pretending to be Satan, put the Crossfire Team into direct conflict with all the forces of hell. After the summation Jack led them into a prayer to Yahveh to give them wisdom concerning their future since the demise of Zagon. They were resting in the Lord when Jack felt the presence of an angelic being. He opened his eyes to see the Angel Caleb standing in the middle of the War Room work area.

Jack smiled, "Hello Caleb my old friend, what news from Heaven do you bring us?"

Caleb was in his warrior image with the bright, glowing robes and the large sword belted around his waist. "Greetings, warriors, The Most High is pleased with the outcome of the conflict between the agents of Satan and the Crossfire Team."

"Since the demise of Zagon and the exposure of the true source of the war against the Crossfire Team, the demonic has reverted to their world-wide efforts against mankind and your team is no longer their primary focus."

"There will be many demonic efforts that the Most High needs your team to stand against in these last days. Marco Marino seems to have decided that he needs to tolerate your interference with his plans. His loss of the RHONE to your efforts and Satan's loss of Molec and Zagon apparently has convinced them that it was not wise for them to concentrate on eliminating your team because you are God's hand on Earth. But, rest assured that both of them will still cause much trouble for your team."

Caleb concentrated on Jack and Mark. "It would not be wise for you two to irritate Satan during the remainder of these last days. He will be quite busy with his prophesied future until the return of Yahshua and he gets a thousand years of rest.

Because your constant onslaught by the demonic forces has now been returned to a normal level, you must collect the Force Generators and put them in a secure vault until the Most High tells you to use them again. That does not include the unit protecting whatever ship you are traveling on at the time. Also, Raquel will return to his normal duties as an Archangel. I personally want to congratulate each of you and the other warriors of the Crossfire Team for your faith and dedication to the Most High and His plans for you."

Later, on a quiet Thursday morning, Jack walked into the War Room and saw Laura. He asked her "What is the status on any new events?"

She sat back in her seat and stared at him. "On the War Room Big Board, there aren't any activities. But on the Carol Report there are several things that will fall into our lap in the next twenty-four hours. At the moment, I don't see anything."

Jack sat down and sighed. "This is like what Mark calls a soldier's life. Long boring periods of nothing interrupted by short bursts of hair-raising, deadly combat. I prayed about this to the Father and I got the leading that this is a short time of rest in Him."

Laura shook her head. "I think I get tenser the longer the quiet lasts. I would rather ..."

An alarm sounded and the Big Board lit up. Jack smiled, "Break's over guys, let's see what we have."

Laura studied the read-out on her monitor. "It looks like we have a demonic element to an assault on the U.S. Naval Base at San Diego, California and it's the Navy that is asking us to get involved."

Another annunciator tone and Jack's screen lit up. He shook his head as he read it. "You're not going to believe this. This is a request directly from the Director of the FBI endorsing the United States Navy's request and guaranteeing us full access and immunity from the U.S. Government on any previous interaction between them and us if we agree to help them with this problem."

Laura laughed, "Yeah, just like the Russian's guaranteed us the same thing and then tried three times to blow us out of the air after we ended the demonic invasion of their country. I don't buy it."

Jack hit the Core Team assembly button.

Eight minutes later all members were there and Jack took a head count. Himself, Laura, Mark, Sarah, David,

Alexis, Christi Steel, Charlie Wu, Linda Wu, Su Li, Mike White, Ethan, Elon, Megan Cole and Carol Moffet. Fifteen seasoned warriors and intelligent people. Jack smiled at them, "Okay folks, we have had some time to rest and it's now time to get back to work. I want a show of hands of the people that are glad about that."

Everyone raised their hands. Jack nodded, "Thought so, all right, here's the drill." He explained the two messages and asked for individual inputs.

Mark started, "I know that the Military likes us and is pulling for us. Still, they have to follow orders and the Marco Marino stacked administration wants us in jail or dead. How can the Navy or the FBI "guarantee" us anything?"Sarah agreed with Mark.

David nodded his head, "I agree with Mark and Sarah but would like to investigate this offer before we just say no. That could really hurt our image with the military."

Alexis seconded the idea of further investigation before they put their lives on the line. "Remember, we don't have the use of the Force Generators at this time."

Charlie looked contemplative, "I would test the waters with a partial team and keep the others in reserve in case there is skull-duggery behind their offers."

Linda shook her head, "I think we should sneak into their computers and find out if the offer is valid or just a ruse to put us in their trap."

Su Li and Mike had no opinions about the validity of the offer. "We will fly you anywhere you want to go."

Ethan agreed with Linda Wu. "I can flush their files but we need to remember that these people are some of the sneakiest dis-information distributors in the world."

Elon added that he could work with the Mossad and get a reading from them. "Many times they possess information other groups don't have."

Megan smiled, "I don't have an opinion either. I will make anything you set up, work."

Christi just sat quietly and listened to the veterans discuss the offers.

Jack thought about the options and sent Ethan, Elon, Charlie and Linda to do their things. He asked Carol to see if she could get Hugo to help her interrogate the Matrix and see if there were any demonic efforts regarding this attack that would include the Crossfire Team. Everyone else began to pray and seek God's wisdom.

CHAPTER TWENTY-FOUR

The majority of the Core Team finished praying and waited quietly for a response from Yahveh God.

Jack thought he saw the angel Rose in his mind's eye. It was so brief he wasn't sure but, when he opened his eyes he saw the angel sitting on nothing in the middle of the War Room circular table.

Before Jack could say anything, Laura greeted the angel. "Hello Rose, how are you today?"

Rose smiled at Laura, "The same as I have been for the last four millennia, Laura. Joyful and ready to serve the Most High. I see that everyone here is the same. Your prayer has come up to the Most High. I have been granted the honor to bring you His answer. Hear the word of God."

"Warriors of Heaven on Earth. You are right to be wary of the offers of guaranteed security and freedom from a service dedicated to the Government of the United States at this time. The offer is given in true faith but the ability to prevent the Government from interfering with your group is limited. Your anointing is needed to prevent a major disaster. Go in My name and be prepared to fight for your freedom anyway. I will be with you as will my messengers."

Rose remained after delivering the Word of God. "I also have a word from Hugo. He says that the enemy is attempting to create a country-wide shakeup by the disaster at the Navy Base. Your help is needed in stopping the terrorists backed by demons. Beware of "Xyctan". He is a demon strong man with control of a legion of demons and he is guarding Satan's desires in this action."

Rose faded out of sight.

Jack thought for a minute. "All right, we need to be wise as serpents and gentle as doves with these people. I am going to take Su Li, Christi, and Ethan with me. I am going to make a tentative visit to Navy Base San Diego. Laura, I want you to lead a backup crew that will include David and Alexis and ten others you select. If possible, before you have to get involved, try to pick up Mark and Sarah."

"Mark, I want you to precede me into the base with a snooping agenda. You need to be in disguise so that you cannot be picked out by facial recognition systems. The same goes for you, Sarah. I want you two in position before the announced visit by my team so that you can cover us. Keep your battle/COMM capability so we can stay in touch."

Jack got out of his seat, "Laura, come with me."

Jack walked over to the R&D group and got in touch with Captain Robert Maxwell, the interface between the Crossfire Team and the R&D group.

Jack shook his hand, "Thanks for seeing me on such short notice Captain Maxwell."

The Captain smiled, "Just call me Rob and we'll get along. What do you need this time Jack? An orbiting space base? A star ship?" The humor was obvious and infectious.

Jack laughed, "No, nothing like that. What I need is a combination of all those things, by tomorrow."

Rob suddenly didn't know if Jack was kidding. "It might take a little longer than that."

Jack shook his head. "Actually, I need to know what you have that has maximum armor and weapons. I might need to break some of my people out of a U.S. Naval base and get all of us home. I know the aircraft we've already used are not armed."

Rob looked at Jack with calculation. "Did we tell you that?"

Jack shook his head, "Nobody ever mentioned it."

The Captain looked into the far distance as he used his forefinger and his thumb to stroke his chin. "No, we didn't, but then you didn't need weapons on those trips either. That entire thing aside, I think we have the platform you need for this trip. It is a little slower than the three you've used so far but it has its endearing qualities."

Jack nodded, "Show us what you've got."

Rob waved for them to follow him. He walked across the hanger to a small personnel door and opened it. After the three of them were inside the very short hall, Rob used a strange key he had on a chain and shoved it into what looked like a crack in the metal wall of the hall. He twisted the key and the hall dropped down two levels very quickly. He turned the key back to the normal position and pulled it out of the wall. He then walked back to the door and opened it. He stepped through followed by Jack and Laura. They were both amazed by the aircraft in the lower level hanger.

Again, the shape was ultra-modern maybe even beyond leading edge. The plane had very slick aerodynamics and was definitely radar-agile, very stealthy. It was three times the size of the Ghost and even its form radiated power and strength.

Jack was awed by the craft. "Tell me what we've got here, Rob. I can see that it can carry a lot. What is it, a bomber, cargo plane, or something else?"

Rob was delighted they appreciated the craft. "Well, it definitely falls in the "something else" category. In 2010 the DOD wanted a stealth aircraft with the fire power of an Aegis class destroyer yet sneaky enough it could slip through an enemy's radar system and park next door to the target without being detected. They never got it but you do. It doesn't have the invisibility that your Force Generator can provide but, it is hard to see and harder to find electronically. It can also take a lot of firepower and not notice it."

Laura asked the Captain, "How many troops can it carry?"

Rob chuckled, "About ten, maximum."

Jack stared at the man. "The Ghost is one third the size of this and it can carry fifty people."

Rob nodded, "While that is true, the Ghost doesn't provide the firepower this one does. This baby has three of the most modern weapons available. It has a targetable blue laser that will melt through a battleship's hull, both sides, in less than ten seconds. It also has a working high power rail gun which will do the same thing in less than one hundredth of a second. It also has the first massive, targetable nuclear cannon. By itself, this plane can destroy one small town every twenty seconds and keep it up for ten minutes. It also has 300 of the Hellfire missiles it needs to destroy a lot of enemy combat aircraft, land targets, stationary or moving. It includes anti-missile missiles, radar disruption weapons like chaff, flares, mini-sun flares, and ten 20mm multi-barreled cannons. One up front, one in back, and four on each side. It doesn't need bombs." He smiled, "Oh, all of this is computer controlled and defended from hackers, EMP, and sabotage."

Laura asked if it was autonomous of if it required direct pilot operation.

Rob smiled, "I don't think we are quite up to the nuclear armed autonomous aircraft just yet. It takes an in-place pilot with command authority over the computers to allow the use of the atomic cannon.

Jack shook his head. "How long would it take for a person to be trained to operate this beast?"

The Captain shook his head. "At least six months, if they were already a trained pilot in modern jet bombers and fighters. But, I get the impression that you are going to have your wife command this air craft. To save her having to meet the training requirements, and the apparent urgency you need it, I will be the pilot, under her command."

Laura, smiled as she said, "Rob, I appreciate that offer and I realize we couldn't have a better pilot, but, have you ever come face-to-face with a real demon which is attempting to kill you?"

Rob shook his head, "No, but you will need something to do while I'm driving the bus. Keeping demons away from me would be a great idea."

Jack shook hands with the Captain. "Can you be ready by tomorrow morning?"

Rob nodded his head, "No problem, I keep my gear on this one. We could be ready to leave in thirty minutes if you need to."

Jack chuckled, "No, tomorrow morning will be sufficient. Thank you Rob, I will feel much better about putting my wife in harm's way with you driving the bus."

Laura asked as they were leaving, "What's the name for this one?"

Rob grinned "Formidable". "By the way, when it is near the ground and in attack mode, inside it is cool and quiet, outside there is a power rumble that does remind one of a huge tsunami bearing down on them. You know, ground shaking and rumbling, buildings falling down, a great deal of oppression, doom, dread, fear, anxiety. Stuff like that pretty much. That doesn't even scratch the surface of what this baby can, and will, do."

CHAPTER TWENTY-FIVE

Jack looked at the determined look in Laura's eyes and stopped her as they walked back to the Crossfire Team base entrance. He turned her around to face him and smiled at her. "Honey, you are more than a conqueror in Yahshua. You'll do fine with the Formidable. If you need any technical help I'm sure the Captain will be able to give you what you need in information. If he can't, then David will be with you."

Laura stared at Jack for a few seconds. "Dear husband, I am not worried in the least about using the Formidable, I have the Creator of the Universe and all of his angels to help me. What I am concerned about is if I can control myself with all this immense power and death-dealing hardware. In my mind this is just about as heady as Holy Anger. Pray for me to do what the Father wants me to do, not what I might want to do."

Jack stood there under a beautiful, if fake, moon in a quiet night and prayed with passion for his wife and the coming battles.

Laura patted his back and told him, "Thank you Jack, I needed to know that I wouldn't lose my control. It is important to all of us."

Jack checked the time after they got back to their apartment. He led Laura over to the dining table and sat on the other side from her. "I'm going to tell you what I think you should do. That is up until there is a need for you to act. At that point it will be up to you because I will probably not be able to contact you. If we are threatened by the Navy, the terrorists, or any other human agency, I won't have my Force Generator, my armor and sword, and any other weapons except my martial arts with which to defend myself. If demons are involved, I will have my armor and sword and will be able to do a credible job of defense. Either way, I will probably need you and your giant gunboat to get us out of a situation."

Laura put her hands over Jack's bigger ones. "Whoever "they" are, they had better not try to hurt or kill any of you. They won't like the results."

Jack nodded, "Remember to keep Su Li, Christi, Ethan, and me alive while you're saving us, okay?"

Laura sat there and ticked items off on her fingers, "Let me see, shall I use the Gigawatt laser, the Rail gun, or the Atomic cannon? I have to be careful to not knock the building down, char it to cinders, cut it to tiny little pieces, or irradiate it until it glows. Hmm, that could be a hard decision."

Jack laughed, "Okay, I'm sure you'll work it out."

Mark rang their door bell and when the door opened he walked in. "I'm ready to take off with Sarah." Jack shook his head, "Who did the makeup?"

Mark looked fifty pounds lighter than normal. His normally muscular shape was almost ordinary. His dark black hair was now blonde and obviously dyed and his face was puffy under his dark tan and thick glasses. Jack really could not identify his best friend. Nerdy clothes and oversized shoes finished his disguise. He walked clumsy and not very coordinated. He thought, "This would work if they didn't strip search him."

Laura smiled, "What does Sarah look like?"

Mark tipped his head to his left. "Hey, sweet'ums, could you come in here for a second?"

Sarah walked haltingly into the Malone's living room. Her dark hair was dull and faded. It was turning to white at the temples and in the center of her head. It was combed back tightly with a bun at the back.

The eyeglasses and the wrinkles at her mouth and at the corners of her eyes and her neck made her look many years older than she was. Her watery blue eyes looked weak and old. Other signs of a long life were the spider veins on the sides and back of her legs and veins on her hands which were also covered with several age spots. She was wearing an old style long dress and a small sweater that looked like she knitted it herself, years ago.

Her hands shook slightly and she didn't seem too steady on her feet when she walked. She had a dignity that let her hold her head up regardless of the ravages of time. Her face was also puffy and matched Mark's face somewhat. She carried a handkerchief and a pair of white gloves in the same hand as her simple black purse.

Laura was speechless. She knew it was just window dressing but, in her emotions, she felt sorry for the older woman's condition and stage of life. Laura applauded, and then she laughed, "I am completely amazed at the conversions. Good job!"

Jack stood up, "Would you two senior citizens care to take a seat?"

Mark said in a crusty rasp, "Watch your manners young whipper-snapper! My wife and I have work to do. We have to leave for the airport to catch our flight to San Diego in an hour. I hope you young'uns will be able to join us tomorrow morning around noon."

Jack shook Mark's hand and noticed he stayed in character by giving him a weak grip and letting his hand drop by his side after he let go.

Laura hugged Sarah goodbye and noticed that she only hugged her back gently.

Jack advised them about the possibility of being picked up by Laura in the support craft.

Mark asked, "How will we know which one is hers?"

Jack laughed, "I doubt that you'll have any problem determining which aircraft belongs to Laura. It's named *the Formidable*."

After the Connelly's had left, Jack asked Laura if she thought the disguises would fool the computers?

Laura nodded her head, "Yes, I do. Did you notice that Mark compacted his body by scrunching down and bending somewhat forward? That reduced his height by at least two inches. Sarah on the other hand added a couple of inches with heels and lifts in her shoes. I honestly would not have known them if I just passed them on the street."

Jack agreed, "Alexis knows how to change a person's shape and presentation. She had to do it to herself and to people she was rescuing or moving in public. I also admire the acting ability of both Mark and Sarah."

He looked at the clock on the wall. "We'd better get some sleep. You've got to get up around 4:00 A.M. to move the Formidable to the Pacific coast off of the Naval Base in San Diego. I've got to be at Ben Gurion airport at

7:00 A.M. to fly to San Diego on commercial air lines. It would be too obvious if I flew in on the Shrew."

After Jack took a shower he set the alarm for 3:00 A.M. and crawled into bed and fell asleep quickly.

CHAPTER TWENTY-SIX

Jack walked back to the Crossfire Team base after the "Formidable" had flown out of sight going out the transit tunnel to the gate under the man-made island. He had to admit that the aircraft was everything in projected power and deadliness Rob said it was, and then some.

He finished packing and met Su Li, Christi, and Ethan an hour later. Everyone was dressed in civilian clothes and looked like average tourists. Ethan patted his bag; "I've got body armor in here but no weapons."

Jack nodded, "We'll pick up what we need while we're there. Either that or Mark and Sarah, or Laura will provide us as we need them."

Su Li looked at Jack, "What was that ominous rumbling I heard about an hour ago?"

Jack rolled his eyes, "That was Laura and the rest of her team in the "Formidable" leaving to be in place when we get there."

Su Li was curious but held her tongue for the time.

Five hours later they walked out of the exit corridor at the San Diego International Airport. Jack rented a car and drove to the base. They checked into the base as tourists and drove to the tour office.

Jack parked the car and got out as the other three joined him. He stood by the car and waited. Christi asked, "Why are we waiting?"

Jack and Su Li grinned. Jack said, "There were facial recognition cameras at the guard shack. I think we will be greeted in a couple of minutes."

He had just finished speaking when two MP vehicles rolled to a halt next to their car. Four MPs got out of the two vehicles and two of the men stepped forward and stopped and saluted. "General Malone?"

Jack stood straighter and returned the salutes. "Yes, I am General Jack Malone."

"The older and sterner of the men asked politely, "Would you and your people please accompany us to the Base Commander's office?"

Jack nodded, "Of course, Sergeant, we would be glad to go with you."

Jack and Christi got into one of the vehicles while Su Li and Ethan got into the other. The ride was short and they got out and walked with the MPs into the Base Headquarters building.

Jack was aware that Naval Base San Diego was a homeport to 54 ships and hosted 120 tenant commands. The base had 13 piers that stretch over 977 acres of land and 326 acres of water. The total on-base population was 20,000 military personnel and 6,000 civilians. It was an awesome facility.

They were led to the Base Commander's office and entered when requested. Jack saluted the Base Commander, Vice Admiral Frank M. Gifford and was saluted by the Vice Admiral in return. They both dropped their salutes at the same time. The Vice Admiral indicated the chairs and said, "Please be seated."

The Vice Admiral studied the four people carefully. "I understand that the Joint Chiefs of Staff have extended a request for your help in our problems out here."

Jack nodded, "Yes Sir, Admiral. I wanted to recon the situation before deciding if we should accommodate the Navy. We aren't on the best of terms with the administration and the Commander-in-Chief."

The Admiral smiled, "Neither is the Navy for making this request. But, they don't have any weapons in their quiver to deal with these supernatural beings and I understand that you do."

Jack nodded, "Yes Sir, we do. Just to clear the air, we fully support and stand with the Military of the United States, always have and always will. Administrations come and go, but the Military still has to solve the problems regardless of politics or opinions."

The Admiral nodded his head. "I am aware of your situation and appreciate your willingness to help us. I am curious as to how you can deal with these beings when no one else can."

Jack thought for a second. "The answer to that depends on two things, your relationship with God and your ability to resist the requirements of Marco Marino to arrest us, detain us, and turn us over to a special group of FBI agents who give their loyalty to Marino over the oath they swore when they became agents to the Constitution of the United States. I'm quite sure that those agents are either already here or they are on their way here."

The Vice Admiral realized that Jack knew the situation and was being open and honest with him. "I am a Christian, always have been and always will be. The five-star Admiral at the Pentagon gave me the authority to defend you and your people to the utmost of my ability and that of my command."

Jack nodded, "Thank you, Sir. Then the answer to your question is this. The God of the Universe, Yahveh anointed us to combat this illegal intrusion of demons, in the physical, into the human dimension. We have been given a physical set of armor and God-powered swords to do battle with the demons. Demons are fallen angels and are stronger, usually bigger, and definitely uglier than normal humans. The armor, shield, and sword level the playing field in our combat with them."

"Admiral, could you give me a general description of what your demonic problem is?"

CHAPTER TWENTY-SEVEN

The Admiral frowned, "We have a dual problem, half demon, half terrorist. A large group of terrorists, approximately one hundred to one hundred thirty men and women have been attempting to attack the base and the ships moored here. Our Security troops have pretty well prevented them from reaching our ships or anything of importance here on base until last week."

The Admiral shook his head. "That's when we began to have demonic problems. These terrorists aren't well trained, armed, or coordinated. But, you add in demons that are apparently indestructible, that attack and kill our troops while we are attempting to stop the terrorists and the terrorist's raids have been getting better. The worst thing is that our Intel analysis of the situation indicates that the real attack hasn't hit us as yet."

Jack nodded, "Thank you for that summation, Admiral. Can your people show us what has happened so far?"

The Admiral stood up and grabbed his service hat. "Come on, I'll show you myself. I'm a little short-handed and I don't want to pull someone off of their attack investigations right now. Anyway, all of the attacks have been in the late afternoon."

Ethan had been quiet the whole time. Now, he spoke up. "I'm sorry Sir, now may not be the best time to expose yourself."

The Admiral stopped, looked at the young man, "Why not, Mr. Reaper?"

Ethan showed him the computer Tablet he was studying. "I'm showing a great deal of demonic activity right now just off shore and approaching the outer ring of the base."

The Admiral looked at the tablet and saw strange swirling symbols. He laughed, "Come on son, we will be all right. I've never seen one of those things anyway." The Admiral opened the door and walked out.

Jack nodded to Ethan, "Good try, but Admirals are the law of the land on a Naval Base." Jack and the others walked out behind the Admiral.

The Admiral was accompanied by four Shore Patrol MPs who were armed with assault weapons. All three vehicles moved to Brinnser Street near the end of Pier 6 facing west. The Admiral exited his vehicle and the MPs got out of their vehicle and formed up around him. There was a Spruance Class Destroyer DD-963 "Walker" docked at Pier 6 and there were sailors moving purposefully around the decks of the ship. Jack could see the steam rising out of the stack on the ship. It was definitely warmed up and ready to sail.

Jack felt the charged atmosphere and stood still. He faced the ocean where he could sense a heavy demonic presence. Christi said, "I don't like this, something bad is headed our way." Jack nodded, "Ethan, contact Mark and Laura and tell them we've got trouble headed our way. Tell them where we are too."

The Admiral stared at the ship moored to Pier 6. He walked over and asked Jack, "What is going on? The crew of the "Walker" looks like they are getting ready to go to war."

Jack turned to the Admiral, "Sir, I respectively suggest that you return to your office immediately. I don't know how the Walker knows what is coming but it is coming and I would feel better if you weren't in the line of fire."

Admiral Gifford shook his head. "Not today son, I want to see what we're up against. I am ..."

A high pitched whine caused Su Li to yell, "Get Down!" as she threw herself at Admiral Gifford and pulled him to the ground and threw her body on top of his. Ethan was going to do the same to Christi but Jack beat him to it. So, he threw himself flat on the ground and pulled himself into a ball. The four MPs followed Ethan's example.

A tremendous explosion blew metal and parts through the air over the little group and the blast beat at all of them. Jack looked up to see a cloud of flame erupt from the fan tail deck of the destroyer. There were several people blown off the deck.

A strident alarm blared from the ship as another whine preceded another blast, this time from the foredeck of the destroyer. This blast blew away from the group of people on the ground three hundred feet away from the stern of the ship.

There were more explosions from other ships that were docked nearby and several inland from the docks.

Jack jumped up and pulled Christi up. He ran to Su Li and found her pulling the Admiral up from the ground. Jack looked at the MPs and told them to get the Admiral out of there and to some form of shelter. There was another massive explosion two dock down from where they were. The concussion was heavy enough to knock everyone back down to the ground. The Admiral yelled at Jack. "That wasn't a missile that was a torpedo!"

Jack looked around and saw a concrete ditch behind them toward the base. He hurried everyone over to the ditch and discovered it was ten feet deep. He jumped in and helped the others down to the bottom. There was a large drainage pipe twenty feet from where they were. Jack ran down to the pipe and waved everyone to him. They moved fifteen feet into the pipe and to a relatively safer place.

One of the MPs was trying to raise their base without any success. "Sir! Communications are down."

Christi turned toward the pipe opening as the ground shook and explosions filled the air. The Admiral was mad, "This is my base." Jack called the general number of the base and got an operator. He handed the phone to the Admiral who started giving orders.

Jack felt the threat that Christi had felt and he turned toward the opening also. The Admiral stepped close to Jack. "Can we get out of here and head toward the headquarters? Its only three blocks from here."

Jack looked at the Admiral with a very serious mien. "Not right at the minute Admiral." He looked at the MPs. "Gentlemen! You are about to see your first demons. This will attempt to freeze you in position. I want you to override the fear and fire at least one shot into the heads of any and all demons you see. If they don't notice your shots, try a different demon. We'll take care of the bullet-proof ones. Admiral, stay a distance behind me. Have one of your men watch behind us."

Jack felt the warning and stepped away from the Admiral and the MPs. He started to pray and his armor, shield, and sword appeared with an explosive blast of light. The Essence of Yahveh was rolling off of his blade in waves. The purity of those waves caused the Admiral and two of the MPs to involuntarily cry out as they waited.

With a solid shaking, two large demons stepped down the concrete ditch and shoved their way into the drainage pipe. Both were typical big, obsidian-colored, ugly, and smelly demons with large black swords.

Su Li engaged the first one and got knocked to the side. Jack engaged it as Christi and Ethan took on the second demon.

The first demon was very quick and eluded Jack's first swing of his sword. The demon used its other fist to knock Jack backward off his feet. He started to rise when the demon stepped on his chest and raised its sword to strike him in the head.

A bright blade appeared out of its chest and it screamed as it began to dissolve into red smoke and spilled demon stain on Jack. Su Li gave Jack the thumbs up sign and headed back to the second demon.

Jack rose to his feet in time to see Ethan knocked over and to the ground. Christi faked a slash to her left and then quickly reversed her sword and decapitated the beast. While the demon turned to blue smoke and collapsed to the floor Christi turned around and stuck her left hand out to Ethan and helped him up. Then Ethan, Christi, and Su Li went to the opening of the pipe and stood guard.

Jack turned back to the Admiral and the MPs. He saw a look of severe astonishment on their faces. One of the MPs said, "We fired at their heads as you told us General Malone. It didn't bother them."

Jack nodded as there was a rapid series of explosions outside and the three team members back peddled away from the opening. Jack stopped praying and his armor and sword faded out of sight. "Thanks guys, God has to give authorization to the enemy to allow demons to enter our dimension. If he does, then bullets and bombs don't bother them because they keep their supernatural attribute of protection. If Satan ignores getting God's permission and moves them into our dimension himself, they come here without their supernatural attributes and they can be killed by bullets or bombs."

The lead MP asked, "What do we do if bullets don't bother them?"

Jack smiled, "Call us." It had grown quieter outside. Jack looked at the Admiral, "I'm going to take a look and see what's happening out there now that the cluster bombs have stopped falling. Christi, call Laura on the Formidable and see if she can find where the naval shells and the cluster bombs are coming from." He moved past the other team members and said, "Stay here and defend the Admiral and the MPs."

CHAPTER TWENTY-EIGHT

Jack checked the ditch and saw that it was empty. He jogged down the ditch until he could look over the wall. He stopped and took a deep breath and felt the pain from where the demon had struck him. Jack covered his chest in the blood of Yahshua and pled the blood the Savior shed at the whipping post. He declared that by accepting that torture and shedding His innocent blood that "By His stripes we are healed." The pain disappeared and Jack quickly calculated the action going on. He turned and ran back to the drainage pipe. He went in and addressed the Admiral.

"Admiral Gifford, there are probably a thousand terrorists headed for the docks in rubber boats. Do I have your permission to engage them?"

The Admiral took a stride and then ran out of the pipe and up the ditch with Jack and the others close behind him. He quickly evaluated the approaching troops and realized his troops would not be there until after the enemy had landed and dispersed. He looked back at Jack. "Permission granted."

Jack called Laura. "Take out all the troops in the rubber boats at once!"

Laura came back with "Roger, will do."

The Admiral stared at Jack. "I think it will be interesting to see you do that."

Jack grinned, "Just watch Sir."

The ground began to vibrate and shake. The Formidable rose out of the water behind the flotilla of rubber boats and suddenly thousands of 20mm explosive rounds flew from the sides, front, and back of the aircraft. All of the terrorists were shredded, several times and the rubber boats were destroyed. The firing took less than twenty seconds. There was probably not enough of anyone left to identify them.

Suddenly a missile was launched from the Formidable and it streaked over Jack's position and there was another explosion behind them. Jack told the Admiral to tell his base defenses to stop firing at the Formidable.

The Admiral relayed the command and the base stopped trying to destroy the aircraft.

The Admiral looked at the huge Warcraft hanging above them and looked at Jack with an obvious question.

Jack shook his head. "It is an advanced mission-specific aircraft, still under wraps. I can't discuss it except to tell you that it has only used its lightest weapons so far."

An MP car slid to a halt on the street behind them. The driver got out and ran to the Admiral. "Sir, the Naval Chief of Staff wants to talk to you." The MP handed the Admiral a cell phone. Admiral Gifford spoke for several minutes.

While the Admiral was on the phone, Jack had Rob land the Formidable and disembark the rest of the Crossfire Core Team. Jack then had him lift off and provide air cover. He was about to go back to the Admiral when he heard Caleb tell him that there was going to be a massive attack by demons in ten minutes.

He got back just as the Admiral disconnected the call. The Admiral was a bit surprised to see ten more of the Crossfire Team standing behind Jack.

Jack didn't mince words. "Admiral, you and your men need to get back to your headquarters right now. There are going to be hundreds of demons here in a few minutes and they only want blood. Go now!"

The Admiral reached out and shook Jack's hand. He and the MPs jumped into the car and took off.

Jack positioned the troops and then saw an old man and woman jogging up to him. He smiled, "Hi guys, you want to change clothes? We've got a few hundred demons coming our way in a couple of minutes.

Mark and Sarah started removing their old folks clothing and putting on their body armor and boots.

Mark pulled out the stuffing in his cheeks and took the glasses off his face, then he ruffled his hair. He really began to look like himself except for the blonde hair. Sarah was even quicker and was fully dressed and checking her M-8 and her extra magazines.

There was a massive snapping, ripping, and screeching sound as a huge horizontal rift opened and hundreds of demons poured out.

Jack told everyone to use the special ammo and grenades until they ran out. After they ran out the team all started praying and acquiring their armor and swords. They moved toward the growing number of demons as Jack prayed that the Father would release His angels to help them battle the huge number of demons.

The battle was joined and the Team held the upper hand for the first hour. Then tiredness and damage began to allow the demons to push the Team back toward the base. Regardless how many they killed there was always more added on the enemy's side.

Jack tried to raise Rob and have him use the Formidable to close the rift but couldn't raise him. The demons, or the terrorists, were blocking their signals.

Jack noticed that there were more than two hundred soldiers, sailors, SEALs, and Army personnel massing behind them and a withering river of bullets, grenades, and rockets flew into the ranks of the demons. That cut the odds down somewhat but the demons kept attacking the Team members. In a massive attack the Team was being shoved backward and compressed into a small space. Many demons bypassed them and attacked the Military units behind them. That was an all-out slaughter.

Jack realized that without the Force Generators his team was about to be overwhelmed and destroyed.

Christi had been destroying demons constantly since they attacked and was tired and frustrated. She saw the inevitable destruction of the Crossfire Team and she prayed, passionately, to Yahshua and Father Yahveh to let her save them. Two demons attacked her at the same time and several more headed her way. She knew that she would be killed in the next minute or so. She realized that she wasn't worried about dying. She knew where her spirit and soul were going. But, it was hurting her greatly knowing she was letting the team down.

She eliminated both of the close demons and determined to take on as many at once as she could until she couldn't fight any more. She sang of her love for the God of the Universe and His Son. Suddenly a thought appeared in her mind. Her strength grew and she killed several demons which made the others leery of attacking her. She took a deep breath and slammed her sword into the ground. She saw the demons charge at her now that she was unarmed. She knew she had to do one more thing before she died. To save the Team she willingly offered up her life. She saw the black swords being raised and she knew without a doubt that she was about to die. She had to do this now! She took a deep breath and with all of her strength she sang a word as loudly as she could.

Being who she was and having years of training in choir and voice, she intuitively used the proper timber, pitch, in the right key register to sing the word properly with all the power her lungs could generate. It was only one word after all, and she was able to give it her best.

The word was unpronounceable on Earth and could only be sung in the correct key and timber. It was a Heavenly word of power. She couldn't believe her eyes as all the demons around her instantly shattered. That was the only way she could understand what was happening to them. They shattered into tiny particles. As the word spread out from Christi it gathered strength. Anything demonic was destroyed completely.

Jack and Laura were fighting to the end, standing back to back fighting ten demons when suddenly the demons begin to disappear. Within seconds there were no demons near any of the Crossfire Team. Jack looked back and the demons attacking the Military units also shattered and disappeared completely. As the flood of incoming demons shattered closer and closer to the rift, a shell flew from the Formidable and into the rift just before the word of power got to it and it snapped shut. Jack had seen the glare of a nuclear explosion as the rift disappeared.

Everyone dropped to the ground as their armor and swords faded out of sight. Laura sat there completely exhausted and asked Jack. "Did the strong man "Xyctan" ever show up?"

Jack shook his head. His neck hurt and he had a raging headache from the battering and energy expenditure. "Not that I know of. But, I think Christi just fulfilled her mission. She surely saved all of our team."

Christi wandered over to where Jack, Laura, Mark, and Sarah sat or lay on the ground. She sat down heavily and leaned back on Jack. "Did we do well?"

Jack reached back and patted her hand. "We did well, and if you hadn't sung that power word when you did, we would be in Heaven, praising the Father right now. All of us. I think you just completed your mission."

An older man walked over and sat down with the little group. Jack looked at him for a few seconds. "Hi Caleb. Where was the angelic backup?"

Caleb smiled, "We were there but we couldn't act. The Most High held us back so that Christi would offer her life as a sacrifice to save you and your team." He looked at Christi and reached over and placed his hand on the top of her hand. "I had confidence in you. I can tell you're related to Jack and by association to Mark. Your use of that Heavenly power word cost the demonic realm over sixty legions of demons and removed a large part of the demonic realm over California. You need to know that there was no one but you, who could have sung that word correctly to save both the Team and the Naval Base."

Christi had been thinking about the fact that she had completed her mission to save the Crossfire Team and what that completion meant to her future as Caleb spoke to her.

When the Angel put his hand over hers she had an epiphany. She literally felt eternity flow through every atom of her being. Her mind was opened to visualize the entire universe and all time. It seemed to last for years as she understood so much beyond the life on Earth and time. It felt like she had been given a direct link to what the Angel Caleb knew and had experienced in the thousands of years of his existence. The experience was much more than heady; it was life confirming, life changing, and a deep knowledge of eternity. She now understood time and wasn't surprised to find Caleb still talking to her on the ground of the Naval Base. One thing she knew for sure was that she had other mission critical events ahead of her with the Crossfire Team.

The Angel looked into her eyes and confirmed that she had received what the Most High wanted her to see and know. When she smiled at him it was a smile of pure knowledge and the love of God. Caleb nodded his head and Christi simply nodded her head back in shared understanding.

Laura asked Caleb, "What happened to the strong man "Xyctan"?"

Caleb grinned; "Xyctan" was bringing another three thousand demons to a new rift he was creating so that they could come in from behind you. Unfortunately, for them, they ran into the Heavenly Host first. Xyctan and his demons, didn't survive the meeting although there was a serious loss on our side as well."

Caleb got up and walked over to where several of the Team was tending to the fallen bodies of Megan and Elon. Neither warrior was responding to their efforts. Caleb gently moved the others aside and knelt down between the two dead Team members. He placed his hands on each person's forehead and spoke to the Most High and asked Him to perform a miracle for each of them. Elon opened his eyes and lay there for a few seconds. Then he grinned and sat up. Megan started suddenly and jumped up into a low posture with her hands in the high guard position. She looked around and realized there were no demons around, she didn't have her armor or sword and lowered her hands.

Caleb waved the other team members back to the two revived members and he walked back to where Jack sat. Jack asked him, "What were the illegal events that Satan did that allowed God to restore their souls within them after they had been killed?"Caleb grinned at Jack, "He did it because I asked him to do it. Membership has its privileges you know." He looked at Jack seriously. "Beware of the people behind the terrorists. They are aware of your participation in the destruction of their people and the demons here. They will seek revenge against you. They are planning an attack against your team, now." The Angel faded out of sight.

Jack turned to speak to Christi about her future and stopped as he saw the awesome depth of all eternity in her eyes. "I am pleased that our Heavenly Father has enlightened you. You look pleased and comfortable in your new knowledge." Jack wondered where that information came from and realized God was speaking through him.

Christi smiled a beautiful smile. She reached over and put her hand over Jack's bigger one. She looked at Jack. "God touched me and I will never be the same. My life is now woven into the pattern of the Crossfire Team's future."

She stopped for a second and then smiled even bigger. "I am so blessed; I have been given a small glimpse of eternity and thousands of years of knowledge. I so want to tell you about it, but, not yet. Be prepared, soon, the whole team will receive this revelation."

CHAPTER TWENTY-NINE

The team assembled and prayed their thankfulness to a loving God and His Son. Jack noticed a distinct difference in Elon's attitude. He was more confident and much more lovingly considerate with the other team members. Megan Cole shared the improvement in confidence in her attitude and she had always been very considerate of others. Jack, in his own small way, approved of their resurrection as far as their improvements. He made a mental note to speak to each of them about their beyond death experiences.

Jack and Mark walked over to the troops that had come to support them. He looked at the fallen troops and prayed that Father God would reward their sacrifice with life in Heaven with Him. Thirty-seven lives had been taken by the demons. The Captain in charge of the counter-attack walked up to Jack. "General Malone, the men and women here have asked me to have you pray for them."

Jack, Mark, and Christi agreed and called everyone together and knelt on the ground and prayed powerfully for all of the troops and their futures. When they were finished, four of the naval personnel came up and sought permission to speak to them. Jack saluted the four and asked what they wanted.

The senior rating was a woman; Erica Simmons was about twenty-two years of age. Normally a pretty woman, at the present she was covered in mud, dirt, blood, and gun powder residue. Her hair was in disarray under her helmet and she still had her assault weapon strapped across her chest with her right hand holding it ready for use. She asked Jack, "We would like to know why you prayed for a future of our fallen comrades?"

Jack smiled at her. "Because death is not the end of a person's life. It is only a doorway to a new existence. Your spirit does not die, it is eternal and when you leave this life you will either go to Heaven to live with God or you will go to Hell and torment."

The woman shook her head. "I don't believe in Heaven and Hell. I think this life is all that you have."

Christi put her hand on Jack's arm. She smiled at the younger woman. "You say you don't believe in Heaven and Hell, yet you fought bravely against demons. Creatures of evil, which belong to Satan. Those supernatural creatures were real, weren't they?"

The woman nodded her head in agreement. Christi then said, "If they are real, then Angels and God are real. Therefore, a pleasant and loving place called Heaven is real."

The woman looked into Christi's eyes and saw the truth of her statements. She dropped to her knees on the ground when she knew in her spirit they spoke the truth and then she sighed, "I have a lot to think about."

Christi stepped up to her and hugged her. As she made contact with Christi the woman's eyes flew open in awe and astonishment. She started to kneel again, but Christi stopped her. "Just like you, I'm only a servant, worship God."

An MP came up to Jack and saluted. "Sir, the Admiral requests your presence at his office."

Jack nodded, "Thank you Sergeant. Wait one, I'll be right there."

Jack told Mark, "Get everyone back on the Formidable and be prepared for anything. I think the Admiral is one of the good guys but he can be overruled by the White House."

Mark smiled, "I'll tell Laura to stand by. I'm going with you." He looked at the displeasure on Jack's face. "Don't take that attitude with me buddy, remember, I out-rank you."

Jack shook his head. "Because Christi most likely just completed her mission, you are again, number one on the devil's most hated list. Don't say I didn't try to protect you."

Mark smiled, "Don't worry about old Sparky, I got this one."

Jack talked to Laura and Rob on his battle/COMM. "You know what has to be done and what to watch for. Congratulations Captain, nicely done on the local warfare and the nuclear farewell to the demonic contingent. I will keep you two in the loop."

Jack and Mark rode with the Sergeant back to the Naval Headquarters building and made their way to the Admiral's office.

Admiral Gifford welcomed them both cordially. "I want to promise both of you that I have never seen bravery like what you and your team demonstrated out there today. Also, I could never have imagined such conflict. Now, I understand what you meant when you implied that the administration is in cahoots with the devil. Look at this."

He handed Jack a flimsy printout. Basically it told the Admiral to insure the safety of the attackers and to confine the Crossfire Team immediately. There were Special Forces in route to take command of the detainees.

Admiral Gifford was irritated. "I am committing treason but I assure you that I will use every resource this base has to defend you and arrest the forces they are sending after you."

Jack prayed for a bit and then smiled. "Admiral, don't put yourself in their bad graces. This base and the U.S. need men like you in charge. Don't worry about us. I so very much appreciated the efforts you and your base staff did to defend us already. Tell Washington that you have tried to capture us but we were too powerful. Play the game and stay in the game. I think we may have eliminated the threat to your base, but, if you have more demonic problems let us know. Here is our private number. We can be here within two hours and I for one would be glad to defend this base and its Commander."

Admiral Gifford nodded his head. "I see your strategy. Okay, you'd better leave before this Special Force arrives and finds us having coffee and cake. I want to thank you for coming to our rescue at the risk of your lives. May God bless you in His Son's Name, Jesus."

Mark spoke up. "Admiral, if you don't mind, I think we will return to the Formidable and welcome the Special Forces right here on your base. Make sure you tell them where you've got us boxed in. There has already been a great deal of damage at Pier 6 so that would be a good place to welcome the new guys. Remember, do your best to show them that you are following their orders, we'll do the rest."

The Admiral asked, "Why don't you avoid the conflict and just be gone when they get here?"

Mark smiled, "Because I want them to see that you really were unable to arrest us and to teach them another lesson. This administration is the most anti-American, pro anti-Christ regime you could imagine, and they need to be put in their place."

The Admiral thought for a second. "If you plan to face them I can tell you that they will use air assets to attack and destroy your aircraft first and then they'll probably use ground forces to like tanks to overwhelm you and force you to surrender. There could be considerably more damage to the base in this conflict."

Mark nodded, "I'm sorry if that is a possibility but we will attempt to keep the damages down and keep any collateral damage to your base and personnel to an absolute minimum. You can bill the Government for anything else. That all right with you?"

The Admiral considered the possibilities and nodded his head. "Just keep you and your people safe."

Mark got a word from God and held up his hand. "Admiral, we can set up your communications so that it seems you are in your office but I believe God wants you with us during this conflict on your base."

The Admiral grinned. "You bet!"

Jack and Mark stood up and took the Admiral with them. They were taken back to where the Formidable waited for them.

CHAPTER THIRTY

Back on board the Formidable, Mark introduced the Admiral who took the role of anon-involved observer.

Mark then laid out his plans for the oncoming battle. "All right Guys, and especially you, Rob. I want to disable these oncoming troops and remove their ability to wage war on us. If possible I want to avoid killing as many of them as possible. Remember, they are misguided by their superiors and think that they are the good guys. We have a chance to impress everyone in the Armed Forces and possibly the uncontaminated parts of the Government by our Christian handling of these aggressors."

Rob was nodding his head when Jack's cell phone chirped. He answered it and heard the Admiral's Aide's voice. "Be ready, the Special Force is coming through the side gate nearest to your location. I make it out to be four main battle tanks and three APCs. There is also a request for several aircraft, two F-22s and three A-10s to overfly the base and engage your aircraft. There are also approximately thirty-six foot soldiers. Let me know if things get too hot and I'll try to arrange a massive distraction." The line went dead.

Jack looked at the others and repeated what the Aide told him.

Mark stood up and said, "It's "Show Time" everyone strap into your seats. Do you need any help Rob?"

Rob shook his head, "No, I think this aircraft can more than handle the forces against us. I will attempt to keep casualties at a minimum." He activated all the combat systems and lifted the Formidable to a hover altitude of twenty feet to allow him more maneuverability.

Rob activated three large vision screens and said, "Here comes the aerial attack."

Jack, the Admiral, and the other Team members watched as the radar picked out the two F-22s vectoring in on their position with a notation next to each plane as to what weapons were selected. The F-22s each showed two GBU-32 JDAM ground attack 2,000 pound bombs.

Jack told Rob, "Render the aircraft incapable of dropping their bombs and then disable them both."

Ron said, "Yes General" and hit three switches on his armaments panel. He took the Joy Stick and aimed two of the multi-barreled 20mm cannons on the left side of the Formidable. He squeezed the trigger and both cannons responded by firing off thirty rounds at each aircraft. At the same time a high powered laser blinded the aiming sensors on the F-22s and shut down the JDAM releases. As the F-22 broke off in two directions to avoid the lasers, the 20mm rounds took the engines and back ends of the two aircraft off completely. Both pilots ejected as their planes went out of control. Rob realigned the Formidable so it faced the oncoming A-10s.

Rob told Jack, "The A-10s will attack us with their 30mm, seven-barrel, GAU-8 Gatling gun, probably using HEI/API "combat mix anti-armor rounds and up to six Maverick missiles and they will be on-guard against the laser attack."

Mark asked, "Rob, can you take out their engines?"

Rob shook his head, "Probably not. But, I can cause them to shut down completely. He changed switches on the armaments panel and used the Joy Stick to select all three of the oncoming aircraft. Rob suddenly deleted the third one and squeezed the trigger. He reselected the third one and pulled the trigger a second time. After the attacks Rob told Mark that he had to wait a bit for the third A-10 to clear the base before disabling it.

By then, the first two aircraft were dropping in altitude and rolling to their left. Both pilots punched out with their ejection seats. Ten seconds later the third pilot also ejected. He had waited until he could aim his aircraft at the Formidable.

Rob switched two switches on his armaments panel and pulled the trigger on the Joy Stick. The Formidable launched two air-to-air missiles which exploded the third aircraft before it could reach the Formidable.

Rob looked at Jack. "If we take on the ground troops there will be a lot more checks in the "casualty" column."

Jack was about to reply when Rob suddenly drove the Formidable backward and upward several hundred yards from where they had been hovering. The video screens showed the six explosions from shells from the tanks below.

Rob immediately ramped up the engines and went straight up several thousand feet. Rob looked at Jack. Jack deferred to Mark. Mark had been praying about the original question. He unbuckled his seat belt and jumped up out of his seat. He tore off his shirt and took off his body armor. He ran over to the doorway of the aircraft and pulled out his combat knife. He drove his knife into the metal doorframe, pulled it out and did it again. He reached into his body armor and pulled out two leads with metal probes. He jammed one probe into each of the holes he'd made. He then reached up and toggled the switch on the body armor. He was relieved when he saw the green LED on the Force Generator. He then switched it to "Special". He put his shirt back on and walked back to his seat. He buckled up and told Rob to go back down to the area of the battle. "You said you wanted to see what it was like to fly a plane with a Force Generator. Well, here's your chance. By the way, the Formidable is invisible right now."

The Admiral shook his head. He looked at Jack. "Are you telling me that Mark's body armor has the power to protect this whole aircraft? If so, why didn't he use it during the battle with the demons?"

Jack nodded, "I'll tell you a little later."

Jack had been praying also and knew what God had told Mark. Yahveh wanted to impress the Military that He is God and not to be trifled with on any level.

Jack spoke up to the other Team members and told them what Mark had been told by God and that they were safe.

Rob said, "Mark, make us visible please. The ground forces know where we are by radar anyway."

Mark went back and switched the FG to "Normal".

Rob said, "There are three F-22s zeroing in on us right now. I expect missiles."

In less than thirty seconds six missiles struck the FG field and exploded. There was no damage or even shaking in the Formidable.

Mark asked Rob if he could determine which vehicle had the Officer in control of the ground forces.

Rob typed in several commands and nodded. "He's in the rear APC."

Mark said, "Use your fun ground effects and park us nose to nose with that APC, wheels up at full power."

Rob grinned and moved the Formidable to ground level and then advanced on the APCs. Men bailed out of the first two units and ran to the sides. Rob knew that the ground vibrations from the power of the Formidable were jellying the guts of those in the area. Since the three APCs were in a line he shifted the Formidable to the left and when the nose was at the right place he moved the aircraft back in line with the third APC. This caused the FG to "nudge" the front two APCs to the right, about a quarter mile. Rob grinned, "Oops". Now the fifty-ton aircraft was literally nose–to-nose with the third APC.

Jack said, "Rob can you connect me to the APCs communications?"

Rob shook his head. "But, come up here and use this microphone and I'll cause the APC to emit your words. It's kind of like the "Big Voice" from the "Chicken Little" movie from a couple of decades back. You know, awe-inspiring."

Jack said, "Do we know the Commander's name?"

Mark sent to a text message the Admiral's Aide. Several minutes later he got a text back that gave him the information. "Major Jed Dixon".

Jack keyed the microphone. "Major Dixon, we need to talk. Please exit the APC and come back to the doorway on the left of our aircraft."

There was no response of course. So, they waited. Eventually the Major opened the rear door and walked around the APC and over to the door of the Formidable.

Jack said, "This could be a ruse, the guy could have explosives on him, or it could be a trick for us to lower our shield and they will fire on us."

Rob typed in a command and then said, "He's not carrying any explosives, not even a hand gun. Remember that the Formidable can handle a lot and I doubt that they have had time to get authorization to use a nuke on Military property anyway."

Mark walked to the door and pushed the switch to open it. It opened and Mark turned off the FG and reached out and pulled the Major inside. He reactivated the FG and walked the Major over to the seating area.

Jack stared at the man. "Major Dixon, my name is Jack Malone and I hold the rank of a one-star General. Would you kindly tell me your orders are concerning us?"

The Major stared Jack in the eyes and recited his rank and his ID number. Jack chuckled, "Okay Major. Then I will tell you what is going to happen here. We are a Team anointed by God to prevent demons from overwhelming humans, even humans that are too ignorant to understand and give all praise and worship to Yahveh God. As you can see, God protects us from all enemies. Thanks to Marco Marino, who is the anti-Christ, the Military of America is tasked to stop us. You do realize that you aren't fighting us, you're fighting against God." We are in the right and we are not going to surrender to you and you are not going to attack us again. Now, how would you like to conclude this conflict?"

The Major repeated his numbers again and fell quiet.

Jack shook his head, "It's too bad you are not allowed to communicate anything of substance. So, tell your tank commanders to get everyone out of the tanks because we are about to destroy the vehicles. I think your APC is the only one left. So, go back to your vehicle send your command to the tanks and get everybody out of your APC. God doesn't want you to use these vehicles to assault us or anyone else."

Mark took him by the arm to the door. The Major shook his head, "I don't believe that you have anything to do with God." Mark turned off the FG and opened the door and showed the Major out. The major took one step and turned around to say something, when suddenly the Archangel Raquel appeared outside the Formidable's door and held up his left hand. A 105mm Armor Piercing Round from the Abrams M1A1 Main Battle Tank deflected off of the angel's hand and flew out to sea where it exploded harmlessly.

The wrath of God was on Raquel's face and his fiery eyes transfixed the Major. "You need to believe. What the General told you was the truth." The angel disappeared and Mark closed the door and reactivated the FG.

CHAPTER THIRTY-ONE

Jack had been praying and asking the God of the Universe what He wanted them to do. He got a leading and called Mark over. "Take out all their war capability but try to not destroy the personnel. If they fight back, God says to destroy them along with their weapons."

Mark went to Rob. "Locate and map all of the Special Forces equipment and individual arms. God wants us to destroy the equipment until they don't have any chance to fight with us. Try to avoid any personnel unless they continue to attack us. They will have made their choice and they will die with their equipment. Can you do that?"

Rob pushed two switches. Another panel in the co-pilot's seat lit up and became active. Rob looked at Mark, "No, I couldn't do that. But, you can." Mark sat in the co-pilot position. Rob showed him which controls and the Joy Stick that selected which weapons.

Rob typed in a serious command and the screen in the middle of the console in front of Mark became active and suddenly there was a map of the end of the base that they were at. Rob added, "When you select your target and approach it, it will be highlighted in a heads-up display on your forward vision screen and you can select one part of it or more as you want to."

Mark told Rob to rotate and highlight the three APCs.

Mark spoke into the microphone, "Major Dixon, if you haven't left your APC you have one minute to do it. It and the other APCs and the Tanks will be destroyed at that time."

The Formidable rose ten feet off of the ground and rotated to its right as it slid to its left. Mark used the Joy Stick and highlighted all three APCs. The side door on the APC flew open and the Major and five men bailed out and ran away from the vehicle.

Mark looked at Rob. "Well, I guess there is nobody there. What do you suggest we do to destroy these three vehicles completely?"

Rob pushed two switches and the three APCs, the one close to them and the other two that were roughly four hundred and forty yards away were highlighted on his windscreen which was, in reality, a vision screen. Mark used the Xaver'Gen III X-Ray system and verified that there were no warm bodies in the three vehicles. He pushed the flashing red button on the Joy Stick and the Formidable launched three Hellfire missiles that destroyed all three of the APCs. Mark was surprised when the first missile followed the other two missiles and then looped up and came down on the APC closest to them.

Rob commented, "It had to reach its effective range and go hot before it could explode. That's about 200 yards."

Mark called the large view up and told Rob to take them to each of the Abram tanks; since they were spread out it would take four different trips. When they reached the first one it fired its main cannon at the approaching aircraft. The shell was defeated by the field. Rob used the big voice and suggested that the troops inside abandon their vehicle because it would be destroyed in two minutes.

Nothing happened for thirty seconds and Mark lit it up with the Xavier Gen III system and saw all four crewmen sitting in their positions and not moving. Rob asked if Mark wanted to drop the tank in eighty feet of water to encourage the crew to leave. Mark nodded his head.

Rob selected three switches and used his Joy Stick to highlight the tank. He then moved the Formidable over the tank and pushed his switch on the Joy Stick.

Mark watched as the Formidable rose into the air with the Abrams M1A1 tank weighing 67.6 Tons rose into the air following the Formidable. Ron took it out over the bay and hovered. Mark used the big voice again to suggest the crew leave before they dropped the tank into the water. Three crew doors opened and the four-man crew jumped off of the tank into the water and swam for the shore. When they were clear, Rob deactivated the lift magnets and the tank dropped into the water with a major splash and quickly filled with water and sank.

Mark aimed the Formidable's main high energy laser at the tank's fuel tank and triggered the laser. The tank blew up and effectively eliminated the tank from combat even if they could dredge it up before it rusted.

Mark's cell phone rang and he looked at the display. It was Admiral Gifford's Aide. "Yes, Major?"

The Major laughed. "I just got a message that the other three tanks are leaving the base to avoid being destroyed."

Mark grinned, "Thank you Major, I just have to disarm the ground pounders and we'll be on our way."

The Admiral quietly said, "May God go with you and your team, Mark."

Rob had moved the Formidable over to where the ground troops were only to finding them loaded into two trucks and following the tanks off the base.

Mark prayed and asked the Lord if what they had done was sufficient to fulfill His command to destroy their weapons. He felt that God agreed. He thanked the Father in the Son's Name.

Rob commented; "Mark you have a visitor."

Mark looked up and saw Raquel the Archangel standing behind him. He swiveled the command seat around and saw Admiral Gifford staring in awe at the Archangel. Raquel saw the Admiral and the Admiral disappeared. "Hello Raquel, now that you have disposed of Admiral Gifford; are we now free to attend to the next immediate crisis?"

Raquel smiled somewhat at Mark's flippancy. "The Admiral is back at his desk and understands I translated him because his people needed him. This information is for your ears only. And as usual, you are looking to go after trouble somewhere, right, Mark?"

Mark shrugged, "I seem to find challenges whenever we get together, Raquel."

Jack spoke up, "How can we serve the Most High, Raquel?"

The Archangel turned and nodded to Jack and Laura. "I came with advice from Hugo. He wanted to visit all of you, but is busy accomplishing the Most High's commands."

"There is a need for your warriors to turn back a second attack by the same group that attacked this naval base. It was planned as a second major strike in a nationwide effort to destabilize the military of the United

States. You were unexpected and definitely stopped the first one, so the second one is being advanced to the day after tomorrow."

Jack frowned, "Does this "group" have a name and a location so that we can meet and greet them in our usual fashion?"

Raquel grinned, "I see that you have been associating with Mark Connelly long enough you are beginning to use his tactics. The group you are coming against was actually a human terrorist organization that has fallen under the control of demons. The group goes by the single name, "Albatross."

Raquel got a look on his face like he had digested something very foul. "This group was an Arab terrorist movement that was ultra-violent and worked on the concept that any man that was not one of them could be a warrior against them. Any woman would produce warriors against them, and any children as possible future warriors. In other words, they kill all living souls to reduce any present or future enemies. No compassion, no mercy, and death are the only responses for anyone other than their own people.

Raquel looked at the assembled Team members. "This organization has been around for almost two decades and is a "shadow" organization that has funded, equipped, and assisted every other terrorist group in the world. They seem to have unlimited funds and soldiers. Lately, they have recruited many of the most violent and intelligent members of other terrorists' organizations or they have recruited potential candidates from the dissatisfied from every nation. They have caused the downfall of several governments and reap the readily available, dissatisfied and demonically driven people that result from the Albatross' destruction of their lives.

"While many of the terrorist groups in the Middle East have regional aims of domination through destruction, death and fear, this group has total world destruction plans and the funds to mount attacks on countries such as the U.S. and Europe."

Mark shook his head, "How can they operate against the control of the Anti-Christ? Won't he squash them using the armed forces of the countries that he now controls, such as the U.S.?"

Raquel shook his head. "No, the Anti-Christ has no interest in destroying them; through Satan, he is in partnership with them. Marco Marino sees their attacks to weaken the military of each of the industrialized countries as a great tool. So that when the second half of the tribulation comes; the One World Government will be able to militarily dictate to all people on Earth because they will no longer have armies to fight him."

Laura spoke up, "Marino might have to rethink that plan before the Albatross eats him too."

"The Most High has warned that this group is going to be the trigger that brings the judgment on the whole world during the three-and-a-half-year period of the second half of the tribulation. This in turn will cause His Son to return to the Earth. Yahshua takes control of the Earth for the next one thousand years. There are less than thirty-two months before the mid-point of the seven-year Tribulation period. To prevent this group from completely destroying all of His children still on the planet, the Most High is using his faithful warriors on Earth to fight against these attacks. To not come against this evil group would allow them to destroy the new and remaining believers who were not saved in the Rapture."

Raquel looked at the warriors steadily for several minutes. "You need to understand that this group will be the sternest test of your commitment that you have met so far. These terrorists are a very competent and smart operation. They have been planning these attacks for the last twenty years. We know that they were about to start their attacks in the year 2001 when the September 11th attacks on the twin towers in New York and the Pentagon stirred up the country and brought the Military to a new level of anti-terrorist activities. The people of the world were behind the Military responses to the Middle East dictators and groups that were, in their own way, behind the attacks."

"To show you the intelligence of the leadership of the Albatross group, they stayed hidden and continued to prepare. They held off their attacks until the people had enough of war and became apathetic. Until the cost of the wars had become too great, and the Military was reduced by an administration with weak and non-patriotic policies. The administration began to pull back their dwindling resources. Then, Marco Marino learned from Satan of this clandestine group and decided to use them and their money and troops to further Satan's domination of the entire world. They have eased their "kill everybody" ideology somewhat to become part of the Anti-Christ's war machine."

"When the world was in financial distress and all the woes of debt and unemployment wore the masses down. Then with their inside help from Marino, they refined their war on the United States. The fact that you were able to stop them is because you are not controlled by anybody but God. Your technology is superior to theirs, but you are few and they have hundreds of thousands of warriors."

Jack nodded his head. "I understand the reasoning, but my question was; can we shortcut having to fight through multiple attacks and go directly after the leadership and heart of this Albatross group?"

CHAPTER THIRTY-TWO

Raquel stared at Jack for a few minutes without saying anything. Jack was pretty sure that the Archangel was talking with Heaven.

Raquel shook his head, "I am sorry, but you cannot use a shortcut. Your Team is intrinsically involved in the Most High's plans to bring about the return of His Son to the Earth. Every time you confront this group and defeat them, they will have to change their plans. This is how God will modify their effect on the populaces of the world and thereby blunt the enemy's attempts to destroy all of God's people."

"Please, understand also that you are not alone. All twelve teams throughout the planet are involved in fighting against the Government's Albatross attacks. I doubt that even Marco Marino understands that the Albatross group is not only planning to destroy the armies of the world. Their desire is still to literally destroy all of the people on the Earth other than themselves. If the Albatross can overcome the militaries of the governments it attacks, it will result in the Holocaust all over again, but far more severe, in all countries everywhere all over the world. Then the Albatross will still turn against the One World Government."

Jack realized that it was the Will of God and he accepted the challenge. "All right, when and where is this new attack going to happen? And, as we defeat them, how far back can we go up their chain of command?"

Raquel thought for a few seconds. "Take out all of their attacking troops, their chain of supply, and the attack command structure. Destroy them completely and their war machines; leave no one alive and no assets to be recovered."

Mark asked, "Humans and demons both?

Raquel nodded slowly and looked at Mark for the next question. A question that the angel knew was coming.

Mark pursed his lips and nodded his head. "Can we use the Force Generators for everyone?"

"The Most High is allowing the use of one Force Generator for the ship. Since you are so few in numbers the aircraft is vital to your operations. In the supernatural world, we believe that unless the demonic efforts are increased beyond your capacities you won't need the Force Generators on a personal level. We will be with you and if God sees that you do need them, they will function. And, so that you won't be distracted by constantly checking to see if they are working, I will tell all of you when they are allowed, if they are allowed."

Raquel continued, "The next attack is scheduled for early morning the day after tomorrow. This is Tuesday and the attack is to occur on Thursday morning at a super-secret facility in the Florida Keys.

Jack asked, "What is the function of the secret base?"

Raquel nodded his head, "It is a drone control facility that can control all of the U.S. drones, worldwide. The Albatross knows about this hidden base and is planning to destroy all of the 12,000 personnel on the base and use the four hundred drones on targets inside the US. They are also planning to capture over fifty bases in the Western Hemisphere where the drones are physically stored and launched. This is a major operation that the Albatross has been planning for four years. They have trained their personnel as well as the U.S. have trained their drone pilots and service technicians at the launching bases. The Albatross will use the U.S. drones to attack their own nuclear missile bases in upper Western States, and other U.S. bases in Canada, Mexico, South America, as well as U.S. Naval forces and ships at sea. They also plan to use nuclear weapons from drones on Washington D.C. by the end of the day. I have placed a list of the other fifty bases that will be attacked, into your electronic devices."

Jack asked, "Why hasn't the Military known about these attacks before now?"

Raquel shook his head. "The Albatross is exceptionally good at secrecy and deception. They have had the help of the One World Government and many traitors in the U.S. Military This attack was so secret that they didn't even announce it to their own leaders of the attack until this morning. I know that the U. S. pressure against your Team will be great when you try to advise the leaders of the coming attacks. But, be careful because there is more than one traitor buried in the command structure of all five of the Military services and they will do all they can to turn the Military leadership against listening to your claims."

Mark laughed, "The Commanders of all the service branches have been fed so much disinformation that we are terrorists that they will do anything they can do to arrest or kill us. What makes you think they will believe us at all until it is too late?"

The Archangel smiled, "Because you have Heaven on your side and we still have good men and women on our side." He faded out of sight.

Mark shook his head. He prayed for several minutes and then told everyone, "Let's get to work. We can't let the press or anyone but the honest people in the military know about this. If word gets out that we are on to their plans, the Albatross will strike early to compensate for our spreading the word of the attacks."

Jack told Rob to head to Florida and then he switched the FG on the plane to "Special" and it faded out of sight itself.

Jack called Vice Admiral Gifford and had him contact them on an encrypted line. When the line was established, Jack checked with Ethan and got the okay. When the Admiral came on the line, Jack told him about the next attack and when and where all fifty-one attacks would be. But, he told the Admiral that nobody in the Military was aware of the pending attacks at fifty drone bases and the main control center in the Florida Keys. Mark also warned the Admiral that there are definitely traitors working with the Albatross in both the Military and the U.S. Government command structures.

CHAPTER THIRTY-THREE

Jack got the rest of the Team to move in as close as possible so that they could use the talents of all the Team members. He looked around at the faithful troops and started. "Boys and girls, we are going to take on a combined human and demon attack with virtually unlimited funds and personnel. Our defense of this base in the Florida Keys will, hopefully, be in coordination with the existing U.S. Military. The other fifty bases will have to make their own stands. I will pray that the Father will assign people from the other Teams to handle the demons in those attacks. If, the Admiral gets the word out and we can convince the security forces and their U.S. Marine backup that we are on their side then we can concentrate on the demons. I have no idea how many there might be in this one attack but I'm sure after the San Diego Naval Base defeat they suffered, there will be many. Listen for Raquel to let you know when the Father will turn on your FGs."

He turned to Mark. "How many people do we have?"

Mark sighed, "Right Now we have a total of ten people here."

Rob spoke up from the Pilot's seat. "If you will get your other troops moving I have called the R&D command and they will get all of your troops and apparently a sizable contingency of IDF and Mossad troops to the Florida Keys before the battle begins. I have arranged the flight with another one of our special aircraft that can carry two hundred and fifty men and equipment."

Mark looked at Jack, "I think we could use a man with Rob's talents in the Crossfire Team, don't you?"

Jack nodded, "Yes, but I'd hate to lose his assistance with the R&D group."

Laura spoke up. "Don't worry, I think he could wear two hats and do quite nicely."

Jack made another call to the Undersea Base and talked to the head of the SOG and to Elon to see how many people they could get to the Florida area in time to help.

Mark made a call to the Admiral. "Admiral, I am going to convince the Command Group at the super-secret Florida Keys base about us and the coming attack. I only need the Commanding Officer's name from you. I don't want to get you in trouble with the head shed."

Admiral Gifford chuckled, "I know Admiral Conners very well, we were cadets at the Naval Academy together and he is already on our side. He watched the attack here and I warned him about the same group coming to mess with him, Thursday morning. He's looking forward to your assistance, I guarantee that."

Mark laughed, "Thank you, Sir. Perhaps you'd like to sit in on this one too?"

The Admiral sighed, "Thank you, but no. I've got to get this base cleaned up and functional. I still have to convince some of my staff that they're not losing their minds. Thanks to your Archangel, I suddenly appeared at a meeting of sixty-three people with no warning. But, I also told Tony Conners that he might prepare for things something similar. Due to my unexpected departure from the Formidable I didn't get a chance to thank you for everything you did, all of you. Not to mention my new paradigm on God and all that. Stay hard and kick their butts!"

Mark thanked the Admiral again and hung up. He told Jack and the others about the "date" the Admiral had arranged for them at the base. Jack nodded his head with a grin, remembering what Raquel had told him about "having Heaven on their side". Very true.

Rob contacted the base for landing permission and, if possible, a hanger to conceal the Formidable until the time for the battle approached. He was routed to a designated space that would allow access to a restricted hanger that was empty.

After landing, Jack took Laura, Mark and Sarah with him to meet Admiral Conners. He directed the other Team members to ask the Admiral's people to get them a place to bunk and showers and then get some sleep. "Keep in mind our relationship with the Washington administration and the possibilities of traitors anywhere. Perhaps a few, willing Team members, would stand watch over the others while they slept. The watchers could rotate and get some sleep themselves." Then he gave Rob an NCO's room by himself, considering the huge burden he would be given during the attack. He needed to be fresh.

Admiral Conners was everything that his friend had said he was. He was a definite command officer and after greeting the four Team members he pulled out three diagrams and started explaining the existing defensive rings for physical defense of the underground base.

Mark agreed with him and described the method of attack the Albatross used on the West coast. Since the island key was surrounded by water it would be a similar attack, probably from submarines.

Mark added, "Since no one but you knows we're here, because the plane was not visible and anyone watching would only see four people coming to see you. They may wonder and report it but it is fairly normal. I am afraid that the attacking forces will probably use missiles off of those submarines to bombard your outer defenses and possible air assets. They won't use too heavy of ordinance because they need your equipment intact to conduct their attacks on the U.S. Are your surface defense points hardened enough to take such a bombardment?"

The Admiral nodded, "We've fortified our outer defense points against missile attacks and planted charges. Now, tell me about these demons. I know that your team will contend with them. But, what do my people do if they encounter a demon?"

Jack smiled, "Well, Sir, demons were once angels, and angels are much stronger than most human beings. What I would suggest is that you shoot them in the head or use a claymore, Anti-tank weapon or something like that on them. If it doesn't kill them then they are impervious to your weapons. We are going to strategically place the Crossfire Team members' through-out your base. If the demon doesn't die, call us, and stay away from them as much as possible. Remember, their goal is to kill, steal, or destroy. That is their whole focus and their life. Our Team members have been anointed by God to fight with and destroy them. I believe that a number of Israeli Mossad, IDF, and Kidon forces have volunteered to help defend this base. They are fierce fighters but they are not anointed and have no more defenses against a demon than your people.

Like your people, they are coming here to defend against the human terrorists that, hopefully, make up the majority of the enemy in this attack."

The admiral sighed, "I watched the videos of the attack on San Diego and I want to tell you all that your method of defending yourselves against the American attacks after defending the naval base against the Albatross attack was impressive. Admiral Gifford told me that while you destroyed over eighty million dollars of U. S. equipment not one soldier, air man, or Navy personnel were harmed. I appreciate your "delicate but powerful" response."

Mark stood up and shook the man's hand. "We can't tell you how much we respect the servicemen and women of America. We've taken our message to the President, the Senate, and other leaders to not waste good men and women of the Services regardless of the desires of Marco Marino to destroy us. It has fallen on deaf ears. But, the American servicemen and women are aware of the situation and they will serve this country regardless of the people who are trying to destroy it."

Jack saluted the Admiral. "Admiral Conners, we are glad to serve with you in the defense of your base. I have to tell you that we will not be arrested or confined by the government and its agents. Please tell anyone that tells you to cooperate because it is your sworn duty that you will. We can take care of ourselves and not ruin your career or reputation."

The Admiral nodded. He stepped back a pace and saluted the four Team members. "We will be ready, and if any self-serving toady of the Government wants to come against you on this island, they will have to go through us first. Let the chips fall where they may."

The four warriors made their way back to the hanger and found a place to sleep. Christi was still up and smiled as she showed them four bunks next to each other. "I thought you'd like a place to drop."

CHAPTER THIRTY-FOUR

Before dawn of the following morning, a futuristic jumbo jet set down quietly on the runway of the island and rolled out to the hanger where the first ten members of the Team were. The one hundred and ninety-six soldiers quietly exited the aircraft and filed into the hanger where they found bunks ready for them. Being in the military a good part of their lives, each one quietly got ready for bed and crawled into a bunk and was asleep in minutes.

Admiral Conners had a late breakfast laid out on tables in the hanger to keep the number of people there a loose secret. Only the security forces knew of the on-rushing attack and everyone else had been told that the new people were reportedly there for training with the defense forces on the base.

Mark set up a large white board and two enlarged photographs of the base. Jack prayed for all of the men and women there and for everyone on the base throughout the battle and any aftermath.

Mark got everyone's attention. "I want to thank each and every one of you that volunteered or agreed to come here to this battle. This one promises to be an epic battle of unknown proportions. We expect to stand against hundreds of terrorists and an equal number of demons. A major advantage we have is that the enemy will not use massive ordnance because they want to have everything in the underground control area in working shape for their plan to work. Therefore, we have decided to make our stand at the eight portals into the subterranean control area. The enemy must face us and defeat us if they are going to achieve entry to their desired goal. Their master plan will not work if they lose the control facility."

Admiral Conners told everyone that the control facility was secretly mined and if the tide turned against the defenders that he personally would push the button and destroy everything in the control facility to prevent the enemy from using it.

Mark stood up and gave Jack, David, and Laura a three-page package of drawings and instructions to hand out to the two hundred plus warriors. "These are the defense zones and strategic power points for defense of the base. Each point has a designated number and contact number for the battle/COMM communicators we will assign to each of you today."

Mark waited until everyone had a chance to look at the maps and instructions. "I am going to have Elon work with your team and squad leaders. Everyone will be assigned a position. In combat, things change and sometimes positions have to change. That is okay; just call it in so that the comm center personnel can keep us up to date on personnel movements. People! This is the only way we can get a Sword Bearer to you in time to take care of any demonic problems. Stay in touch. I will assign Sword Bearer positions while Elon and your leaders make their assignments. We plan on having the Formidable make a severe dent in the number of human combatants before they get to us or even onto the island."

Mark surveyed the men and women facing him. "I am also going to post ten Sword Bearers in the bunker below. While that may seem like a cushy job, let me remind you that supernatural beings do not have to use the stairs to get there. They can materialize directly in the control center. If you believe in God you may see Angels here to help all in the combat. Please! Don't shoot the Angels, it is not polite and they are here to help us defeat this attack. If you have questions, ask us or Elon. I recognize most of you from the battles in Tel Aviv. Thank you for recognizing the importance to the whole world that this battle represents. Pray, serve, and stand in God's love."

After Mark completed his presentation, Rob walked over to him and shook his head. "I cannot believe the strength of faith that brings this multi-national collection of warriors here. I know what I'm going to do is critical to the success of this mission but I feel it's unfair that I can sit in total comfort and security and deal death while everyone here will be in direct one-on-one combat with men and fallen angels. I will be praying for everyone here during the combat."

Mark shook his hand. "We're counting on you. And realize the amount of trust the Father is placing in your hands by letting you use the Force Generator."

Jack got everyone's attention and held up a rifle magazine. The tips glowed with the essence of Yahveh God." The team members from our base brought this special ammo with them. If you see a demon, load this ammo and shoot it."

Rob suddenly looked at Mark, "What are you going to do without your body armor? That is what is providing the Force Generator for the Formidable, but doesn't that leave you without one in battle if the Father authorizes their use?"

Mark looked up at Rob with a small smile. "What makes you think I can't use my body armor and the Force Generator it contains?"

Seeing the confused look on Rob's face, Mark laughed. "Not to worry, I got my armor this morning and replaced it with a belt unit version of the Force Generator brought by our base personnel".

Rob shook his head. "You couldn't possibly get into the Formidable without my transmitter. It hasn't left my pocket and even if it did, the alarm would have sounded."

Mark grinned, "That is true, but neither one of those requirements prevents an angel for making the swap."

Rob smiled back, "Oh yeah, there is that." He was relieved that his defenses hadn't been penetrated, at least, not by a human. Then he realized that if an angel could do then so could a demon.

Everyone spent the rest of the day resting, or working on their weapons. Jack presented new, high level sword training for the Sword Bearers while Mark and Sarah passed out the communicators and a new handgun with a laser for each of the troops. Then a short night of sleep, if possible, and rest otherwise.

At 0400 hours in the morning, everyone was dressed for war and moved out to their locations. After they settled into the best defense they could, depending on their force point, the waiting began. This was the tough stuff, waiting for a larger force to attack them.

The Formidable remained visible as a visual and visceral encouragement for the troops as Rob rolled it out and then took off. The huge aircraft rumbled mightily as it made its take-off. It was more than impressive for those that had not seen it or understood the power it held. As it lifted off it faded out of sight and became silent. It was 0530 hours when the first sounds of the battle were heard.

CHAPTER THIRTY-FIVE

Rob reported over the battle/COMM to Mark. "I detected the approach of eighteen submarines and was detected by the first three. Four anti-aircraft missiles were fired at the Formidable from the first and second subs. Missiles detonated on the FG field without effect."

"I simulated a crash descent and drilled the first submarine with a rail gun depleted Uranium round. I then accelerated out of the local area. The first sub had considerable damage and I believe it sank with all hands on board. I am returning at extreme altitude and observe that the submarines are spreading out to approach the island from multiple headings. Formidable out."

Mark replied, "Good work Formidable, keep us appraised as to the movements of the submarines. Rob, do you have any ASROC capabilities?"

"Rob replied, "I have the three main weapons but they were not specifically designed for anti-submarine warfare."

Mark told Rob to keep watch and inform him of any new developments. He advised the Admiral of the opening shots. "Admiral, I am concerned about this approach via submarines. It's too slow and open to counter attack. Tell your radar operators to watch for low and slow aircraft, especially any of large size that could carry parachute troops."

The Admiral concurred and Mark was about to check with Rob again when there were heavy explosions near all eight of the entry portals to the buried control center. Rob called in with information. "The subs are firing missiles from underwater, targeting the entrances."

Mark checked with the troops at the portals and found that there were some minor injuries by flying debris but nothing serious.

The Admiral advised Mark that a large flight of low and slow aircraft was approaching the island from the Southeast with an approximate arrival in twenty minutes.

Mark called back. "Admiral, advise the aircraft that they are approaching a restricted zone and if they don't alter course they will be fired upon." Mark switched to Rob's number. "Rob, there is a large flight of aircraft coming at us from the Southeast. If they don't break off immediately, take them all out."

Rob acknowledged the order and mapped the flights and targeted them all. He selected missiles to start with and the 20mm guns for mop up.

The Admiral called Mark. "I have permission to open fire on the submarines and I have launched eight aircraft with ASROC capability."

Before Mark could answer, Rob broke in, "Admiral, tell your aircraft to watch out for fighters coming from the North. I have an eight plane flight of fast movers headed at the island. I will prevent them from attacking your aircraft if you want me to do that."

The Admiral agreed with Rob. "I order you to stop those fighter aircraft from attacking my aircraft. They are obviously going to disregard the restricted zone and that makes them legal targets."

Mark concurred, "But, make sure that the fighters don't distract you from the troop carriers."

Rob chuckled, "The Formidable is more than capable of handling both sets of aircraft."

The Admiral replied, "You might want to watch your six Rob, two of the fighters are swinging to their left to attack you right now."

Rob said, "Thank you Admiral, I've got them targeted and will eliminate them first."

Mark and Jack watched the large video screen in the hanger as the two enemy aircraft broke left toward the Formidable and then exploded before they could fire a missile. The remaining fighters scrambled in different directions and altitudes to overwhelm the Formidable only to suffer the same fate. Four of the eight aircraft went down in flames but the other four managed to avoid the Formidable's missiles and stayed on target for the Navy's anti-submarine aircraft. Rob had to take care of the slower flight of troop carriers.

A huge explosion slammed into the FG field as Rob lined up his attack on the troop carriers. He reported that one of the submarines had launched a large missile at him but it had no effect on the Formidable. He stared at the radar. "Hey Mark, these troop transports were using an old technique to hide their numbers by flying several close to each other so that the radar would count five aircraft as one big blip. There are over eighty to one hundred massive troop carriers spread out over a half-mile wide globe. I have only enough missiles for fifty of them and I don't think I can destroy the rest with my Gatling guns. I'm going to have to use a nuclear air explosion to get them all."

The Admiral responded. "Rob, don't do that. I don't have permission to detonate a nuclear device. Just do the best you can with conventional weapons."

Rob replied, "Yes Admiral, I understand. Be aware that at the relative speeds I will still be leaving you with approximately forty aircraft dropping troops on the island."

The Admiral concurred with the estimate. "Then we'll have to handle them the old way. I launched four fighters to contend with the enemy fighters so try not to knock them out of the air along with the anti-submarine group."

The sky over the island and to the Southwest became a whirling battle zone as missiles and gunfire decimated the first wave of troop carriers and twelve fighter-bomber jets competed to live through the battle. Two of the anti-submarine fighters were destroyed but they managed to fire two ASROC missiles before being hit. Three of the enemy jets were hit and knocked out of the fight. Two of the island's interceptors took after the lone enemy fighter while the other two anti-submarine fighter-bombers launched eight more ASROCs at the submarines which were also firing missiles at them.

The Formidable shot down forty-eight of the troop carriers before the flights passed each other. Rob spun the Formidable around and quickly overhauled the slower aircraft. Multiple air-to-air and surface-to-air missiles hit the FG field and exploded without effect to the Formidable. Rob called in the forty-five troops from each of the enemy troop carriers were parachuting out of roughly fifty aircraft over the island. Rob continued to shoot as many of the empty troop carriers out of the air to prevent the enemy from reusing them. Rob reported to Mark that there were approximately two thousand troops headed their way.

CHAPTER THIRTY-SIX

The entrenched ground forces used heavy machine guns and rifle fire to counter the attacking troops from the troop carrier aircraft. The battle was on three sides of the base and the barbed wire and open areas slowed the attackers down and made them subject to the withering firepower from the base defenders. The attackers were using rifles and rifle-propelled grenades as well as shoulder-fired missiles to knock out the defenses as they moved forward toward the six attackable portals. The fighting was fierce and the casualties were mounting on both sides when the Formidable and five of the fighters from the base started strafing and bombing the attackers.

Jack was praying for the protection of all the people defending the base when his armor and sword suddenly appeared. He used the battle/COMM to alert the Crossfire Team that there were demons incoming. He nodded to Mark and headed to the Control Center.

As he entered from the hidden underground tunnel he saw dozens of demons attempting to eliminate the twelve Team members which were defending the underground center. Jack joined the melee and kept blocking black blades and attacking demons constantly. Three demons attacked him at the same time. Jack could battle two of them at once but that left the third one free to smash him to the ground. His armor kept the blow from killing him but it hurt and hindered his defense. Which he had to admit wasn't too effective lying on the ground. He blocked the first stab but knew he wasn't going to block the counter blow due to the pain in his right shoulder and arm. As he raised the sword as best as he could he saw two radiantly brilliant blades take the head off of the third demon and come out of its chest. He saw Laura and Christi behind the remains of the demon as they turned to take on more demons. Jack prayed for the strength of God to empower him to continue to battle against the darkness that threatened to overcome him.

A black boot stomped on his chest and he twirled his sword blade and amputated the leg from the grinning demon above him. He just didn't have the strength to get off the floor. David Zahavy cut a demon in half and reached down and grabbed Jack's hand. David pulled him up off the floor and winked at him.

Jack realized he must have been hit harder than he thought as he couldn't maintain his balance very well let alone a constant defense and attack. He looked around the huge room and saw twice as many demons as he had before he got hit. He prayed that God would provide help for them in this moment of dread. All at once dozens of angels appeared and started battling the demons alongside the Team members. Jack tried to compete with a pair of demons only to be knocked to the ground again. He realized that there was another Team member on the ground and two angels were being beaten down by multiple demons. He cried out to the Father to help them and he heard Raquel say, "Your Force Generators are active now." He reached up and turned the FG on. He still hurt but he felt a renewed spirit and energy. He was able to stand and he cut down demons as he went to the aid of the fallen.

Jack cut two demons in half that were attempting to kill the Team member on the ground. Jack saw that it was Megan Cole and she had blood flowing from a head wound. She was still conscious because her armor and sword were still visible. He leaned over as another demon slammed its sword into his back. He didn't feel the blow because of the FG field. He swung his sword backward to the right and saw the blade cut into the head of the demon that had hit him. He ignored the demon as it fell and dissipated into blue fumes. He then bent over and activated Megan's FG and hauled her up off the ground. He looked at her as five or six demons tried unsuccessfully to kill them. "How are you doing? Are you up to fighting some more or do you want to sit this one out?"

Megan looked at him with pain evident in her eyes. "Could I get a short break first?"

Jack nodded. He looked around and found one of SOG women and asked her to take Megan back out of the area and guard her. As they walked off he turned back to the two angels only to find them gone. He blocked a black blade and started killing demons as best he could. The pain was less than before and he fought but favored his right side somewhat. Three of the terrorists came into the underground control center and started shooting at the Team members and the angels. An Archangel appeared and killed all three of the men.

Jack kept taking out demons and finally saw that the Team and the angels were winning. There were fewer and fewer demons in the control center. Finally, the last demon was killed and Jack's silver armor and his sword faded from view. Raquel announced that the Force Generators were inactive again. Jack saw motes of light floating before his eyes and he felt faint again. He staggered over to a knocked over chair and righted it and sat down.

Most of the warriors were sitting on anything they could find. Some of them were lying on the floor. Jack took a deep breath and called Mark. "The demons are gone from the control center, how is the rest of the battle going?"

Mark responded, "It is over for now. There are none of the attackers alive and the whole island is littered with bodies and weapons. We lost over sixty men and women to the attacker's loss of roughly five thousand troops. They lost sixty-eight aircraft and four or possibly six of their submarines to our loss of three aircraft and two APCs. Were there any injuries or deaths in the battle with the demons?"

Jack sighed, "No losses thanks be to God. But, there seems to be a bunch of injuries, including to Megan and myself. I hope that there isn't a follow-up attack. I think I'm out of it for a while."

CHAPTER THIRTY-SEVEN

The actual count was fourteen injured during the battle with the demons. There were forty-six Navy and Marine deaths from the island defenders. Fourteen of the Israeli volunteers had been killed. Considering the thousands of enemy combatants that had lost their lives it was definitely to be considered a victory. Still it was disheartening to have to take some of the troop's home in body bags.

After checking gun cameras and eye-witness reports the enemy had lost eight submarines, sixty-four aircraft, and four spies. The spies had been uncovered fighting for the wrong side and were summarily executed during the battle.

Mark, Jack, and Laura were sitting in the Admiral's office, counting the damages and working on a report to the Israeli Government. Reports from the fifty other bases were similar except that the drones from six of the bases were stolen before the attackers were repelled. The key to the entire battle, of which nothing was reported to the public, was that the attack was a defeat to the master plan of the Albatross group.

The Admiral was enthusiastic in his appreciation of the efforts of the Crossfire Team and he was equally unenthusiastic in his lack of appreciation of the failure in the intelligence communities which included the NSA, CIA, FBI, and other agencies for their complete ignorance of the Albatross group and their attack plans. After the battle at the San Diego Naval Base it was inconceivable that they would still be in the dark about this group, let alone not figuring out that another attack would be coming. He personally shook everyone's hands and congratulated them for their efforts and faithfulness to a country that was so antagonistic against them. The Crossfire Team and the Israel warriors took their fallen comrades and flew back to Israel on the Formidable and the even larger "Orca" aircraft.

Jack spent a half a day in the whirlpool bath in the medical facility at the Sea Base before he felt basically back in shape. He had to admit that covering himself in the blood of the lamb that was shed at the whipping post did most of the healing. He thought about the two operative comments concerning that healing. The first was "By His stripes you are healed." And "It is finished" There was a lot of prayers of thanks and love to the Creator of the Universe and His Son that evening. Raquel visited Jack and Megan and prayed for each of them to remove any demonic curses attached to them when they were injured. Raquel did a general healing prayer for all of the other Sword Bearers for the same purpose.

CHAPTER THIRTY-EIGHT

Christi was attending a gathering at the Sea Base to study the Bible as seen through the Jewish Roots of Yahshua. It provided so much more depth to the Scriptures that Christi wondered why she ever settled for the first level of understanding.

Twelve of the women of the Crossfire Team were there with her. She was familiar enough with who was who, now that she felt confident in knowing who they were and what they represented. She casually looked around and saw Laura, Sarah, Alexis, Megan, Linda Wu, Su Li, and five woman warriors from the SOG. She had the irrelevant thought that this was a women's group a person would be wise not to mess with. She had fought alongside of every one of these "Ladies" and knew their grit and determination to fight for God.

Christi listened as Laura taught classes on their Jewish roots that were first taught by Senior Pastor Larry Huch at his church in Dallas about the seven things that Yahshua had said on the cross and the deeper meaning of every statement. Viewing it from a Jewish prospective made so much more sense and when the words or comments were coupled with other things from the Bible it completed the understanding of what was actually meant by each statement. It was very exciting and she looked forward to each class avidly.

Laura said, "Okay then, what Yahshua meant when he said *"lama lama Sabatini"*. "It wasn't Father, Father, why have you forsaken me" as interpreted by most of the Christian church, rather it meant, "Father, Father, this is why you fortified, strengthened, or empowered me." So that he could take the sins of the world on his back to free us from our sin burden. Since many ancient Hebrew words often have two meanings, usually opposites, both of which can define the actual meaning of that expression. Also remember that Yahshua demanded a drink when he said, "I thirst". As a Jewish Rabbi he was required to drink four cups of wine at Passover. He had only drunk from three cups. He had not completed the ceremony there at the Last Supper. He would drink the fourth cup, the "cup of completion" in Heaven as he had told his earthly disciples. He said, "It is finished". Let's pray and thank God for the understanding."

As Christi prayed her thanks for the understanding, a strange thing happened. Her eyes were closed and she felt a great peace in her heart. All sound ceased and she felt refreshed and vibrantly alive. She opened her eyes and beheld a marvelous sight. She was sitting on a rock stool looking out over pastures and gardens that stretched to the horizon in all directions. The cool light felt soothing to her skin and the gentle breeze flowed over her like a smooth mist of sweetness and happiness. Her soul felt satisfied with a peaceful love and wonder.

She looked to her left and she saw a dwelling. She knew not to call it a house. It was a dwelling, a place where the spirit stayed for a while in comfort and then moved on to the next adventure. She rose to her feet and walked through the lush grass that felt pleasant to her bare feet until she stepped up onto a cool stone walk that led to the dwelling. She noticed that the stone looked like a very lustrous pearl. As did all the other stones of the walk.

She came to the door of the dwelling and it opened as she approached. She walked in and felt a satisfaction that sang of her being there. It was exactly right that she was here at this time. She drank in the wonderful air and it felt like the most wonderful drink she could ever drink.

There was a fascinating décor to the single room that also looked exactly right. Nothing was out of place or misplaced in the room. There was a single padded seat near a window and she walked over and sat down on it.

It seemed like she sat there only a few minutes when she felt a presence and turned to see a man in a pure white, linen garment. He was about six-foot-tall and had dark hair that fell in ringlets to his shoulders and matched his beard in color. He was darkly Middle Eastern like many men in Israel. He was smiling at her and she could feel the happiness and humor he radiated. She felt her heart ache because he smiled at her. It was like she had done something right and he was glad. That made her so happy she started to cry. He walked over and stood next to her.

He bent over, took her hand in his and stared into her eyes. There were so many more emotions rushing through her than she could express. Somehow, she was very aware that this was the most precious moment in her life.

He spoke to her, "*Precious child, I love your spirit and I wanted to give your soul rest after the all the battles of your young life. Know that our father and I love you and are proud of your faithfulness and your service for us.*" His voice was so exactly right she knew without doubt that He was Yahshua, her messiah. She kissed his hand where it rested on hers and saw the scar on the back of his hand. That brought sadness to her heart because of the pain and suffering he had endured for her. She saw and felt another deep stream of the eternity she had felt with the angel Caleb before. But this time it was more complete and intrigued her even more than before.

Christi slid out of the padded seat and knelt before her messiah without a prayer or a sound. No talking, just silent adoration and love. He put his hand on her head and she felt joy and had a flash of an exciting future.

Yahshua drew her up to her feet and looked deeply into her eyes. "*Stay solid in your faith and know that you are never alone. Our Father and I are always with you. There are great works in God's plan for you and you will be both a warrior of great power and my messenger of hope to many people in the years ahead.*" He turned and walked a couple of steps toward the door. "Come, walk with me." The door opened and he led her out of the dwelling. The beautiful grasslands and gardens were gone and Yahshua showed her a vision of planets with the sun blazing in the void. He brought her down to the Earth and showed her the world to come. She recognized many of the things she had seen when Caleb had led her on a similar vision.

Yahshua told her, "Walk proudly in My Righteousness because your future is bright."

The vision and Yahshua faded from view and she came back to the classroom where she had been praying.

Everyone was gone except for Sarah. Christi looked at Sarah and saw her new friend and mentor in a much more meaningful way. She smiled slightly and said, "Thank you for being there for me when I needed it."

Sarah smiled at the humble yet confident attitude Christi displayed. "I've "waited" several times for Laura when she was taken to Heaven. Then I had a vision and Laura waited for me. It is almost like a rite of passage for the people of this Team. Did you find what you weren't looking for?"

Christi grinned at the flippant comment and nodded her head, "Yes, I did. Yahshua met me in Heaven and I totally fell in love with him all over again. Strangely, I remember wishing that you were there with me even though it was so intensely personal. I want you to know that I love you Sarah. You are the life-long sister I never had until I met you."

Sarah asked about how she felt about Laura. Christi laughed out loud. "She is like the older sister I never had. It's funny but I don't have to wish for a brother or a mother since I have both of them here."

They both got up and Christi turned out the lights in the conference room as they left.

CHAPTER THIRTY-NINE

Mark walked into the War Room and sat down near Jack and Laura who were working the various contact lists and data sources they had to see what they could find out about Albatross as an organization. There wasn't much information available.

Mark told them he had unearthed a little information but only peripheral hints and speculation. Jack sat back and prayed for a visitation from Hugo, their training Angel.

Rose swirled out of a flowing cloud of fierce white and cool gold colors. She smiled slightly at the Crossfire Team warriors. "Hello Jack, Laura, and Mark, I have come on behalf of Hugo who is very busy right now." She looked around and asked, "Where are Sarah, David, Alexis and Christi? They need to be here for this."

Jack looked at Mark who shrugged his shoulders. Mark called David and the other three women who all showed up quickly.

Rose had floated quietly until all seven people were present and then she opened with, "Warriors all, I salute you as you honor the Most High." Then what she said shook the group of people. "The reason I asked you to have David, Alexis, and Christi as well as Sarah at this meeting is because Satan hates Jack, Laura, Mark, and Sarah sufficiently that he will insist on having the Albatross make your elimination very important to them. If they do overcome you four, then David would have to take over as the leader of the Team here on Earth along with Alexis as his wife. Christi needs to know also, that if that should occur then, she is the Most High's back-up for David and Alexis Zahavy."

Laura looked at Rose with concern. "Rose! Are you saying that Jack, Mark, Sarah and I could be killed fighting the Albatross?"

Rose looked at Laura who she saw as a true friend, "There is a possibility, but it depends on many variables as you are aware. Don't let your heart be distressed Laura,

160

you are coming to Heaven in the next thirty-two months anyway."

Laura sat there stunned. She realized that they would only be here until their own Rapture and that prospect was wonderful and didn't bother her. Rose was right! This is what she wanted and they looked forward to the event. The difference in time was not important. That was old time thinking, worrying about dying and leaving this Earth. Laura realized she was looking forward to going to Heaven. Peace settled back in her heart and she relaxed and smiled.

Rose outlined the history of the Albatross since the First World War up until today. Mark asked her, "That sounds a lot like the Bilderberg's history and parallels Marco Marino's One World Government. Is there a direct connection?"

Rose nodded her head, "They are known by many names but their goals are always the same, World Domination, reduction of the world population, complete control of all financial institutions, international and local as well as the military."

She looked at the people in the War Room, "This prophesied world control group has deliberately followed many paths to reach where they are today. They also have a well-designed plan to remove the Military control from the Military. Your appearance has thrown their plans into a knot. But, perhaps you now know what their resources are. The entire subjugated world and all their acquiescent army, naval, and nuclear forces. That is who you are up against. I am sure that they will soon have the permission to use a nuclear weapon to destroy you, your base here, or anything else that could eliminate this team from hindering their plans."

Christi smiled, "Yeah, but we have God on our side. They lose."

Rose grinned at the youngest member of the group, "Well said, Christi, that motto is also what God's plan is too."

"From now on the Most High has this to tell you. Now, hear the word of the Lord." "*My warriors, the enemy of God is now fully revealed in the operations of the One World Government and the Albatross which is their Army. Your Team's destiny will now shine forth as I command. The slow development of the individuals and the technology of the Crossfire Team have reached their peaks and will be the rock on which the enemy's might will be shattered. Use Dr. Clashire to ensure that everything you have is covered by my spirit which will protect you as it does with the Force Generator. Even then, this evil group will use everything it has to break through and eliminate you. Stand brave and walk in my anointing as you contest with the best and mightiest the world has to offer to Satan to eliminate you all.*

Do not be deceived by anyone, even past friends. The combined military forces of the world will be added to the evil hosts of demons to change prophesy, kill believers, and to control everything in their quest to rule. I will stand with you as will my angels, and forces of which you have no concept, yet. I love you and will never forsake you or abandon you. You have My Word."

Jack sat there for a few minutes. Then he looked up at Rose. "This is our ultimate battle before the end of the known world. I praise Yahveh God and Yahshua, His Son, the Savior of the world. They have seen this battle coming for all of eternity. This is where truth and lies collide and truth will emerge victorious.

Rose smiled at them all. "To complete victory in the name of Yahveh and Yahshua." She disappeared in her normal swirling pattern.

Jack sat there and prayed for a while. He noticed that the others in the room were doing the same thing. He got up and went to his apartment and started making phone calls. The first call was to Vice Admiral Conners in the Florida Keys Base. Then he called the Prime Minister of Israel. Next he called Iris Jakobson, the Director of the Mossad. Then the most important call was to Doctor Clashire. Then he sat back and prayed for wisdom.

Three hours later he called a complete Crossfire Team meeting. When everyone was there he presented a short summary of his concept for fighting Satan's demonic empire and at the same time fighting the military of, basically, the whole world which was being ruled by the Anti-Christ. That excluded both Russia and China.

"I have been greatly concerned about our responsibilities to the Nation of Israel and the danger to their existence by our simply being here. The OWG now feels the threat we pose to their drive to dominate or decimate the militaries of their world is too great. Because of that threat they will resort to any means to destroy us. There is no doubt they know about this base and how Israel defends it. There is only one method of attacking us that would stand any chance of succeeding and that is using nuclear weapons. Because Yahveh God protects us, I doubt that will work for them. The problem is that they might destroy a good part of Israel and God's people in the attempt."

Laura shook her head, "Probably not, He protects His people too."

Jack looked at Laura, "While that is true, never the less, I prayed that God would give me the ability to resolve this problem for us and the Nation of Israel. I believe he has let me see His solution and I want to share it with all of you. Because it affects all of you, as well as Israel.

CHAPTER FORTY

Jack smiled at the group knowing that no one there had any idea of what he was going to propose. "Eight years ago, the United States began a secret project to design and produce a limited number of stealthy assault ships for the U. S. Marines. These ships were known to only a few people. As clandestine operations, or Black Ops, the project had the code name of "Dagger". An apt name considering that they were to carry a complete, multi-functional Marine assault battalion with limited air support. This radar-agile, stealth ship could carry all the troops and their support vehicles, and several aircraft. A battalion consists of three rifle companies, one weapons company, and one Headquarters and Service Company and is normally commanded by a Lieutenant Colonel. This was a new conceptual design that would allow quick reaction by an entire battalion of Marines and their ground, sea, and air support. A complete Marine mini-base as it were. The project had progressed to the point that the first ship completed sea trials before the project was abandoned due to cost overruns and a decision to use large aircraft to move the quick reaction teams rather than bringing the entire base with them. That was decided because the majority of quick reaction operations where lasting less than three days."

"At that point the Marines had a problem. They had a secret eighteen and a half billion-dollar project that no one knew about and they could no longer use. The decision was made four months ago to scrap the single ship that had been stopped just short of being commissioned. But, they had no way to recoup the billions of dollars they spent and no way to account for the funds. The present administration would have been unforgiving of the dollars being used without their tacit oversight and permission."

"One solution was to sell the boat to a friendly nation and quietly forget about it. There aren't too many friendly nations for the U. S. to choose from any more. So, they made a back-door offer to Israel. Israel liked the idea but weren't sure they could project such a force in a world where they were not a sea power to begin with. So, with the help of some of our friends and the Nation of Israel, I just bought the ship. It will be a good base for the Crossfire Team that will not bring our heat onto any country. The ship will be here in Israel in two weeks."

"I propose we move our base onto the ship and make that our new home. We will let the word leak out that we are not based in any country, but on this ship. This will remove the probability of attacks on Israel, while seeking to attack us on this ship."

"Now, to answer the obvious questions, which I had to answer for myself and others, I want to explain how this will protect us and Israel, and serve as a well-known, but untouchable base."

"Father Yahveh has granted us a great deal of leeway on our use of the Force Generators created by Dr. Clashire. I have discussed this change with him and he is designing a Force Generator for the entire ship. I am going to integrate the R&D department as the official Air Force of the Crossfire Team. They are one of the reasons I looked for something that would allow use of some of their air craft in our new base. This will further remove Israel as a target for our aircraft while keeping their operation and people safe. We will be able to house two Fragments, two Myths, two Ghosts, and the Formidable. The remainder of the R&D operations and aircraft will be at a hidden base in the Pacific Ocean."

"Israel is still our nation and will be the Country of Origin or Flag Country of the ship. None of our normal relationships with the Nation of Israel or their agencies and their Government will change except that it will take a lot longer for face-to-face meetings."

"As a note of interest, the same vision systems we enjoy here were used extensively throughout this completely windowless ship. The basic stealth design that is used on the ship was based on the "Sea Shadow" a 10-personexperimental design of a small stealth ship that was used in the James Bond movie of thirty years ago, "Tomorrow Never Dies". The "Dagger" class is an Assault Ship and not an aircraft carrier. It looks unlike anything you would expect an aircraft carrier to look like anyway. It is perfect for their research vehicles which should be right up R&D's alley."

There were several laughs at that point.

Jack continued with his concept for the future base of the Team. "We will be hunted and easily found. We will not be destroyed or sunk because we will have continual protection not only by a Force Generator field, but by God Himself and His angels. I expect that we will be tested continually by the Albatross group but that keeps everybody else safe while they focus on us."

"I expect that we will need to make the move to the ship in about two to three months after the refitting. Until then we will fight from here."

He looked around, "Are there any questions?"

Ethan Reaper asked, "Are the communications wiring and routing equipment up to our requirements? Also, are the transmission and detection gear still on the ship?"

Jack deferred to Charlie Wu. Charlie stood up and spoke so that everyone could hear him. "Jack asked me to make that determination. I made a clandestine visit to the ship. I will state that I was more than impressed; I was awed by the cutting edge systems that remain on the ship. When we connect up our CRAY computers we should have one of the fastest and versatile communications and detection systems in the world."

Ethan laughed, "You mean the CRAY Titans at 17.59 PFLOPS?"

Charlie nodded.

Ethan smiled, "Actually, we just finished installing the new CRAY Ultramas at 52.25 PFLOPS. They are smaller and require a 3X increase in electricity but they did include an equivalent increase in cooling capability. They are so fast they give you the result you need before you finish asking for it."

Charlie shook his head. "WOW! That is a giant increase in speed. You should be able to do a thousand times more in one second than you could with the Titans."

Jack interrupted, "They will be moved to the ship in the first week. Charlie, will both you and Linda please help Ethan get them up and running as quickly as possible. Considering the costs, I want full time military security. I am going to assign ten, no, twenty of the SOG as rotating oversight and Sword Bearers in the event the enemy realizes that ship is ours."

David spoke up, "I would ask Elon to get an exterior guard rotation of IDF personnel which will give any watchers the belief that the ship is a normal Israeli operation."

Jack nodded, "Make it so. Also, let the IDF know that our people will be inside, out of sight, but immediately available in the event they run into any demonic problems."

Jack commented on the electrical capability on the ship. "One of exciting things with the Dagger Class is that there are three nuclear reactors installed and available with our licensing. The power output with each reactor providing 104 MWs of power or the equivalent of 140,000 shaft HP."

"The ship runs on one reactor. The second one is for all other requirements. The third one is a reserve marked for future increases in power needs. Think you can find enough electricity to run the COMM/SEC department off of the third reactor? How much power did you say you are going to need for cooling?"

Ethan smiled, "That is no problem. The Ultramas come with the cooling capacity of twice their own requirements."

Jack nodded his head. "On another note, there are no direct visual windows on the ship. Everything is presented on a Viewport or Image screen. That will include the new extensive Atrium and sports/exercise area. All power requirements are triple redundant in case of attack or a power failure of one reactor. Are there any more questions?"

Alexis asked, "What does the ship look like? And what will be its name?"

Jack shrugged his shoulders. "I can't tell you because I've never even seen a picture of it as yet. It has a unique segmented set of surface areas for receiving and launching of aircraft. To maintain its stealth capabilities, including satellite observation the pads change angles when there are no flight operations in progress. I was told that it also can do a chameleon like change and look like the water it is moving through when seen from above. I think the Force Generator field will do better than that when it is in "Special" mode. The majority of the ship is actually underwater and that is where the aircraft will be stored and worked on."

"The name hasn't been selected as yet. The ship will be a detached part of the Israeli Navy and is flagged as Israeli. I think we will have an Israeli name for it. I'll let you know as soon as it is adopted."

One of the aviation avionics techs asked, "General Malone, does this ship have a landing and takeoff deck similar to a normal aircraft carrier?"

Jack shook his head. "No it doesn't have a thousand-foot-long deck; the whole ship is only seven hundred, seventy-seven feet long. This unit only handles VTOL or Vertical Takeoff and Landing aircraft. The nice part is that all of the R&D aircraft we use already have VTOL capabilities. The planes are assigned to a certain "Pad" which serves as the reception and launching pad for that aircraft. One reason the top of the ship is rounded and angled is to keep the ship almost invisible to radar; but, its extensive length is partly to accommodate aircraft like the Formidable."

There were no more questions and the meeting was dismissed by Jack.

Mark and David came over to Jack. David offered, "Well, that should reduce the time needed to get home after an action." Mark grinned, "I'm glad that the Father will allow us to use the Force Generator because we can sleep better not hearing the bombs bursting in air."

Jack smiled at the two men. "R&D's "secret base is being prepared underground as we speak on Victor Chamberlain's island. He graciously offered to use a space the group that had taken over his island had prepared for some operation that never happened. R&D gets five times the space and security courtesy of Victor."

CHAPTER FORTY-ONE

Two weeks later the disguised ship was delivered to a huge covered military dock in The Port of Haifa which is the largest of the three Israeli major international seaports. It is a natural deep water harbor which operates all year long and handles a large number of Military ships.

Jack, Laura, Mark, and David were the first to arrive and examine the ship. It was almost disappointing in its military color and presented a drabness and lack of a dramatic exterior. Mark laughed when Laura commented on the ugliness. "Laura, it is a Navy ship to start with and it is designed to be as featureless as possible to enable it be invisible to radar. Bumps like a Lido deck, swimming pool, and control island would show up on radar instantly screaming "Carrier!" That is why it isn't "ugly". It is just being efficient."

Once they got inside the long ship things were different for the new owners. The rooms were still Navy décor but not so bland. Jack looked everywhere he could but finally ran out of patience. "I need a more practiced eye to check out this seven hundred and seventy-seven-foot-long ship."

They had just gotten back to top of the boarding ramp when a voice shouted out, "Ahoy, permission to come aboard."

Jack looked over the side and yelled back, "Permission granted, Admiral." Vice Admiral Conners bounded up the ramp and snapped a salute. The three one-star IDF Generals and the two-star General snapped to attention and returned the salute. Jack stepped forward and shook the middle-aged Admiral's hand. "Welcome aboard, Captain." He introduced the Admiral to David Zahavy who hadn't had a chance to meet him during the Florida Key battles.

The Admiral looked out over the ship and made Laura frown at him as he said, "She's a beauty". Mark put his hand on Laura's arm and whispered, "Beauty is in the eye of the beholder." She nodded and kept her comments to herself.

The Admiral took them on a whirlwind tour of the ship's four levels and pronounced it fit and seaworthy. Then they found a table in the mess hall and talked about the schedule and the refitting. The Admiral smiled at Laura. "It looks like I'll be just a Captain and not an Admiral anymore. Can't have an Admiral unless you've got a fleet and this appears to be our entire fleet."

Jack took a sheaf of papers out of his briefcase and handed them to the Admiral. "I'm afraid not, Admiral, I have had some friends mainline some paperwork for you."

"In the next two weeks you need to leave sufficient time in your schedule to get your Israeli Citizenship and meet with the Israeli Navy Commander in Chief for a brief ceremony to welcome you as a Rear Admiral in the Israeli Navy. The rank is mostly ceremonial, based on your record of service and combat in the U.S. Navy and our need of you and your capabilities."

The Admiral sincerely thanked Jack for arranging the consideration and agreed that he would make time to see that it was done. "You know, I only had three more years to serve in the U. S. Navy, but I was disgusted with the new direction Marco Marino was taking the services. I want to thank you for giving me this chance."

Jack nodded, "You're welcome and you're needed to make our new fighting base ship-shape. I understand you did five years on carriers before being promoted to Vice Admiral. You should enjoy this service. How many officers and seamen do you need to take care of something this big?"

The Admiral grinned. "This baby is a modern miracle of high tech and automation. A ship this size, with nuclear power, would normally need three hundred officers and two thousand seamen. I will only need fifty officers and three hundred and fifty seamen. Do we have a port of call that can do normal maintenance repairs and upgrades?"

Mark spoke up, "Admiral, you're standing in our only port of call so far. I think they have a much more secure port but it's not open to us until she is inspected, approved, and commissioned."

Admiral Conners shook hands all around and didn't ignore the women. He had seen them fight demons and men alongside of the men. He rated them right up there with the men. He stepped to the top of the ramp and saluted the Team as a whole.

As the Admiral headed down the dock, Mark asked Jack, "How are we going to separate the Team business from the crew business?"

Jack smiled, "That is part of the refitting. We will be in a separate area that can only be entered by medallion and a bio-mass identification. I've assigned David, Alexis, Megan and three trusted Mossad engineers to oversee the refitting and make sure it's done to our specifications. I think that David is intelligent enough to let Alexis and Megan run the show.

CHAPTER FORTY-TWO

Jack knelt next to his bed in their apartment in the Sea Base and prayed for God's protection of Israel and all its citizens and all members of the Team and every action needed to be finished was done before the new "base" was complete and they were aboard. He listened and felt the leading to be at ease. God said that He would see that all was well.

Jack got up and walked out of the apartment and down to the operations floor. He then made his way to the Crossfire Team Synagogue. He entered and sought out Rabbi Joshua Epstein. The Rabbi greeted him and asked how he could help.

Jack smiled at the Rabbi and asked him if they could talk for a few minutes. The Rabbi nodded and walked with the Leader of the Crossfire Team to a table where they could sit and talk.

Jack sighed, "Rabbi, I came to tell you that the entire Team will be abandoning this base in about three weeks. I would like to ask you to pray..."

The Rabbi broke into Jack's statement. "Pray for the men and women? Of course I will."

Jack liked the man's enthusiasm. "No, I want you to pray and see if God would want you to go with us. We are moving our base from this bubble under the sea to a large military craft that rides on the top of the sea. It will be much safer for the Team and the sailors and officers than we are in this base, but it will also protect Israel by our not being here."

The Rabbi blinked several times and asked Jack to come back in an hour or so. This would give the Rabbi time to pray and seek God's direction. Jack agreed and got up to leave. Before he got to the entrance of the Synagogue the Rabbi called out after him. He stopped and turned and the Rabbi ran up to him. "Yes."

Jack smiled, "Yes, . . . what?"

Rabbi Epstein looked at Jack, "Oh, I'm sorry; Yes, I will go with you. I apologize. I was somewhat rattled by the answer I got so quickly from Yahveh God. As soon as I asked Him for direction, He commanded me to do it."

Jack nodded and told the younger man to get packed in the next three weeks because they would be gone for quite a while. "We will be physically separated from the rest of the mixed Israeli and American crew and officers manning the ship. But, I am going to have a Synagogue built in both areas of the ship so that you can provide services to everyone if they want to attend. Is that acceptable to you?"

Rabbi Epstein nodded his head. "Of course I need to pray about that. How many of the crew is Jewish?"

Jack smiled, "We haven't assembled the crew as yet so I don't know the mixture. But, after we run into demons I think most of the crew will also want to seek God.

The Rabbi smiled, "Okay, when will we be leaving and where are we going?"

Jack said, "About three weeks and then he pointed to the west. "We are going to go that-a-way."

Jack returned to the Sea Base in time to be told that the head of the Mossad half of the Sea Base wanted to meet with him, the Prime Minister's office called for him, Elon wanted him to speak to the head of the Kidon, and Christi asked to speak to him.

He sat down at his position in the War Room and sent a message to Elon and one to Christi, scheduling a meeting with each one for later in the day. He asked the Mossad base director to come on over and see him immediately. Lastly, he called the Prime Minister's office and took care of a small problem with the Admiral's paperwork. The Citizenship Panel wanted the correct spelling of Admiral Conner's name. Jack realized that things were moving so fast that no one else had the correct listing of the Admiral's name as yet.

Jack prayed often seeking the Father's will and trying to ensure that the lull in combat with the Albatross and the devil was real and not a tactic to lure the Crossfire Team into a false sense of security. He came away with the leading that the two opponents were preparing to find and attack the Team. Jack wanted to get away from Israel before they could attack. This lull in their life continued for the two months it took to refit the ship.

The next three weeks were hectic as everybody worked long days and nights to get everything moved over to the ship and working. Admiral Conners told Jack that he would rather be known as Captain Conners so that there would be no confusion as to who the Captain of the ship was. Mark vetted all of the officers and seamen before the Captain interviewed them. Sarah assisted Mark and so did Laura concerning the new crew's spiritual baggage and blessings. Only seven percent were turned away by the Team. Thirty percent didn't make it pass the Captain's interviews. They had their crew and the ratings above them who actually ran the ship as directed by the Captain. All of the men were seasoned seamen or women who had at least four years of duty on military ships.

The final crew selected was seventy percent Israeli, twenty percent American, with the remainder primarily British and European. The Security group was almost totally Israeli. The lone rating that was different was Irish and technically British but he was a dedicated, super competent former U.S. Navy Seal. Mark checked him out and determined that he had also been in the British SAS for four years. He did some hard digging and found out that Hugh Kelly had been approached three times by spy organizations but turned down their offers because he was a third generation Navy man and told them that he had the sea in his blood.

Since the ship was officially in the Israeli Navy, Hugh Kelly received the rank of Sgan-aluf or Commander. The Admiral turned Captain Conners had both the official rank of Aluf-Mishne or Captain and Tat-Aluf or Rear Admiral. There were other ratings that matched Lieutenant Commander, Petty Officer, and Seaman. The crew was seventy-five percent male and twenty-five percent female. Everyone from the Captain to the Petty Officers had a major crash course in their specialty. They, in turn, trained the seamen. The normal four month trainings were accomplished in less than three weeks with a lot of detail to be completed at sea.

Jack and Mark responded to a call from David to tour the refitted ship and they showed up an hour later. They liked the work that had been done. Mark especially liked the steel bulwarks that separated the Crossfire Team and the ship's crew. If you were in the Team domain, you couldn't tell that there were other people on the ship unless you were approved to leave domain "T" and entered domain "C". This was done on purpose to prevent leakage of Team business. The electronics and communications were totally separate and could coordinate by a third system. As a new arm of the Crossfire Team, the R&D group was housed in the "A" domain. They had part of their group housed in the "C" domain to handle the aircraft launches and retrievals.

There was only one portal between the T and A domains and the rest of the ship and only the Team members with their Medallions could use the portal. This wasn't done out of superiority or class. It was done strictly for security of unit intelligence and priority. The only people on the ship that weren't team members but could access domains "T" and "A" were the Captain and the ship's COMM/SEC group Commander, Hugh Kelly who also functioned as the Executive Officer or second in command after the Captain.

In one day, Jack and Laura finished moving out of the Sea Base and onto the ship. R&D would move that night and the next night to stagger the movement of their aircraft to the ship at sea, away from prying eyes at the Port. They also moved their personnel at night and that included any laboratory equipment that they hadn't already moved to the ship.

CHAPTER FORTY-THREE

The team arrived at the Port in Haifa and was lined up outside the ship on the dock. Jack spoke to them as a group. "Team mates I present your new base and home to you. Welcome to the "Kherev" which is Hebrew for "Sword". It is pronounced "Kear" and "rev" in Hebrew."

One of the workmen pulled a rope at the bow while another one did the same at the stern and the name was revealed as a third workman raised the Israeli flag on a temporary staff near the back of the deck. It would not be shown when the ship was underway. There was a small picture painted on the hull under the name for normal identification."

The Team boarded up the gangway carrying only a few items. Everything else had been trucked to the Port and loaded yesterday. Each member of the Team was given a room number with directions as to deck, aisle and cross reference so they could find their rooms in their part of the huge ship. The crew had been on board for most of the last three weeks learning their jobs and testing the equipment.

After getting settled in and having a tour of the facilities the Team gathered in the large mess hall which also served as their conference room. Everyone was introduced to the Captain and the Sword's COMM/SEC and Executive Officer, Commander Hugh Kelly.

Jack and Rabbi Epstein then officially blessed the ship and its crew. Then Jack turned to Hugh Kelly. "Commander, is the ship secure and ready to leave port?"

Commander Kelly saluted, "Yes Sir, General Malone. The ship is secure and all hands are on board."

Jack took a key out of a polished wood box. "Commander, Activate the Force Generator field."

Commander Kelly accepted the remote electronic key and moved the guard over the Master Control button and depressed the button. To the team, the slight tingly feeling all over their body was a familiar sensation. The Captain and the Commander stopped for a second and analyzed the feeling. Then the Commander hooked the key onto a metal loop on his belt, stepped back and saluted the General. Jack returned the salute. Kelly turned to the Captain. "Captain, the ship is secure.

Jack turned to the Captain. "Captain Conners, the Team is on board. Take the ship out to sea." They saluted and the two officers left the room and exited through the portal from the "C" domain into the "T" domain.

Then, the majority of the Team exited the portal and stood on the deck and watched as the ship was freed of the dock and moved out of the covered area before moving slowly pass the other ships in the harbor, and finally moved out into the Mediterranean Sea where it picked up speed. Most of the Team had shipped out on Military ships before but were intrigued by the lack of shudder and vibration as the sea waves hit the boat.

Jack used his battle/COMM and called the troops inside to cut down any possible satellite identifications.

Mark made his way to the bridge and was given permission to enter the bridge. He walked up to the Captain's seat and enjoyed the magnificent view of the sea in all directions. He was aware that there were no actual portholes or windows anywhere on the ship. He saw the dedicated vision screen showing the Sword moving through the light sea waves. An auxiliary monitor showed the view from a security drone about a thousand feet above the ship.

He turned to the Commander and asked him to move the second switch on the master key fob from the "Standard" setting to the "Cloaked" setting.

When Hugh moved the second switch even he gasped. The entire outside of the ship had simply disappeared. He walked to the side entry that allowed the bridge personnel to visually monitor the ship by standing on a small flat area outside, on either side of the bridge. He opened the door and stopped. He couldn't see the hull and tentatively put his foot outside the bridge and felt the invisible wing under his foot. He bravely stepped outside and stood on nothing he could see. He looked in his command tablet and selected the drone view. He could clearly see himself, standing on nothing as he sailed over the sea at about ten knots. Shaking his head, he reentered the bridge and pulled the door closed and secured it. He grinned at Mark, "Bloody impossible, but I like it."

Mark grinned, "I thought you would. How do you like your sleeping arrangements?"

Hugh grinned back at Mark. "Best sleep I've ever had, Mate, especially in port."

Mark nodded, "Wait till you try it tonight."

The Captain showed Mark a small screen with a green colored display. "When the Commander stepped outside it turned Red, which meant that the cloaking coverage was broken."

Hugh said, "Now, all we need is an actual Star Ship."

The three men carefully tested all the other functions of the Sword and found them working. The Captain asked Mark, "You still want us at those coordinates at 2200 hours tonight?"

Mark nodded, "We will retrieve and store three of the aircraft tonight and give the R&D personnel a chance to get acquainted with their rooms and the rest of the ship."

That operation went along with only one hitch. At ten minutes of 2200 hours, the ship was in the invisible mode when they came to the position that they were supposed to meet the aircraft from the Sea Base. The crew had been watching a small fishing boat with a crew of five men at that exact position. The Captain advised Jack of the situation. Jack had Ethan exercise the new CRAY computers and check the boat for explosives, guns, or anything else harmful. Ethan came back in less than two minutes. "That boat has a motor and a single flashlight with a dead battery. No sign of weapons unless they have demons hiding them. No sign of demons either. I think they're clean."

Jack gave the fishing boat condition to the Captain. Hugh checked with Mark and then deactivated the Cloaked setting, allowing the seven hundred and seventy-seven-foot-long, forty-five-thousand-ton ship to suddenly appear a hundred feet away from the fishing ship. To say that the fishermen on the sixty foot, twelve ton fishing boat were startled would have been a major understatement. The crew of the Sword had to help them rescue one of their people who had thrown himself overboard when he saw the Sword looming over their little boat.

Accepting the suggestion of the Security Officer Hugh Kelly, the smaller craft hoisted anchor and motored away as quickly as possible. All six planes from the Sea Base set down vertically on the deck, one at a time, where the deck had lit up. Then they were quickly lowered into the lower part of the ship and moved to their positions in the internal hangers.

In less than twenty minutes all of the R&D aircraft were stowed aboard and the Sword disappeared again and sailed out of the area of Israel.

Captain Maxwell of the R and D Group showed up at the new War Room and dropped into an empty seat next to Jack. "Hi there, General." the Captain said as he sketched a salute.

Jack returned the salute and chuckled. "It's a good thing all of your aircraft are primarily lifting bodies that don't need big wings or we'd have to fold them to get them into the hull. Then he asked the Captain what had happened to cause all six aircraft to come at once.

The Captain laughed. "I don't know what you told the Mossad boss about our schedule but I was just getting the first three aircraft ready to go when they demanded entrance to our part of the base. I asked why and they told me that you had said that we would be completely out of there tonight and they wanted to start working on the area. I could see a big argument starting up. To prevent bad feelings, I just pushed my guys and girls and we threw everything we were going to pack tomorrow into the planes and gave them the keys to the place as we left. That is why you got all six of the aircraft tonight. The other thirty-three aircraft and all of the lab equipment have been received at our new secret base in the Pacific Ocean.

Jack breathed a sigh of relief at that point. He prayed his thanks to Yahveh and Yahshua for everything and protection for them and the Nation of Israel. Then he looked at the Captain. "Was it your choice to move all six of the aircraft or did it come suddenly as a good idea?"

Captain Maxwell thought for a little bit. "You know; you may be onto something there. Originally I was going to stonewall them. Then the concept of preventing bad feelings by just going came to me. Note, I said, it came to me."

While Maxwell was sorting out his feelings about the concept, Jack asked him, "Rob, you also told me that you had thirty-three aircraft and we apparently have six more than you told me you were going to bring to the island or here. Why is that?"

Rob actually looked embarrassed. "I'm sorry about that. Originally, in the states we had seventy-two but some crashed, some didn't work out, and some were used as parts for other aircraft. What I was aware of, but forgot, was that the people working for me are very creative and industrious. On their own time, they took all the parts and pieces from the other twenty-some aircraft and started using those parts to make six totally new aircraft that were never scheduled nor reported. Guess how surprised I was when all six of them could actually fly. I liked what they had done and sent them along to the island. I'm sorry that I didn't remember to tell you about them. Oh, by the way, I agreed to help the IDF and the Mossad with their new aircraft like we had been doing in the Sea Base. I hope that was all right?"

Jack nodded, "That was what I told them also. If it gets to be too big of a favor, we might have to tone them down by asking them to pay for some of it. We're not using their money for your operation anymore."

Five of the Crossfire women came into the War Room and said hello to Captain Maxwell as he was leaving. He had been married once and he could see storm clouds on the way in the faces of the women and he decided it would be best if he got back to his group. He noticed that jack grinned at his hurried exit.

CHAPTER FORTY-FOUR

Jack asked the women to sit down and pray with him. They all did and he let them bring their problem before the Lord and helped them pray for an answer.

He looked at the group and realized it included not only his wife but also Sarah, Alexis, Megan, Linda Wu, and Su Li. That was a wealth of talent. "How can I help you all?"

Sarah started off with, "Well, I understand that we are on a military naval vessel but we've come to a consensus that we need to improve the inside décor."

Alexis picked up the gauntlet, "We want your help in getting the rest of the men to go along with us."

Su Li added, "And we need somebody else to do it because all of us, men and women are under a lot of stress to just catch up with what we already have to do."

Laura smiled at Jack, "We don't want you to feel that we are ambushing you, but, we are. You know what the problem is doing to our morale. It keeps interfering with our activities and that will spread to every man and woman in our Team. If you're willing to entertain a female upgrade, then maybe we can turn this thing around before it gets worse. Also, Megan knows who can do this for us."

Jack thought about the opportunities and the drawbacks. "I'm willing to entertain the thought of beautifying the personal spaces. Have you considered that to maintain a legal basis we all agreed to have this ship be a part of the Israeli Navy? They have rules and regulations." He was about to keep going but everyone started talking at the same time in an ever escalating volume of irritation about the rules and regulations.

Ethan started to walk into the War Room but heard the hubbub and decided to let the Generals work it out between themselves.

Jack raised his voice over the noise level. "AS I was saying," this brought the talking to an end. "I am willing to consider your request, regardless of the Navy regulations because we are not an open fleet line ship. We are rather an exception. How is this source that Megan knows, going to be able to help us?"

Laura was somewhat chagrinned and pointed at Megan. Megan nodded and looked at Jack. "I have a good, but arm's length friendship with one of the senior planners for Gary Danning. When we thought of trying to improve the décor here I put in a call to him, only to find that he has resigned his commission and left the service. Fortunately, I was able to track him down through another mutual friend. He's working as an upscale independent contractor in the public sector. Long story short, I got to talk to him and he is interested in helping us if we can get permission. It seems that our reputation was established before because he worked as Gary's main supervisor. You've actually met him and even shook his hand before, General Malone. His name is Bill Franklin, and he was specific that he would not work against you, or Mark, ever."

Jack recalled the man; he looked like an Army Special Ops type of person. He kinda looked like Mark only taller and more bulked out. "Find out what his terms are and then, let me talk to him. If he is agreeable, I will contract him to do the work. He needs to be able to get solid qualified people that can pass our review and inspection. Tell him that I am interested in the project and I will guarantee him and his workers safety and pay."

Everybody jumped up and shouted. They then mobbed Jack and gave him hugs and kisses until Laura shouted, "That is entirely more than enough!" They all backed away from Jack and apologized to both him and Laura. Jack smiled, "Ladies, please remember I am your Priest and my wife is really good with her sword." His grin took the sting out of his comments.

At first all of the other girls looked with apprehension at a frowning Laura. Then Laura couldn't keep the act up and broke out laughing at the looks on their faces. Even Jack laughed with them. "Okay, ladies, two requirements, first, I want to know all your proposals before Bill does. And two, this cannot interfere with your jobs or any operations, fair enough?"

They all agreed and surged out of the War Room talking a mile a minute. Megan held back. "Thank you Jack, I'll get Bill to call you. Do you want to talk to him tonight?

It is only 1500 hours (3 P.M.) in the afternoon where he is."

Jack okayed the call with a caution. "Remember, while Bill will be in charge of the rebuild, you will be our representative responsible for him and his crew. Keep a watch on their activities."Jack sent her on her way but called her back before she got out of the room. "Did the other women do a number on me after I agreed or was that spontaneous happiness?"

Megan smiled a small smile, "I'd consider it actual enthusiasm possibly tainted by a little strategy."

Jack laughed, "Thank you for your honest answer and opinion, Megan." Megan nodded and ran out of the War Room to catch up with the other women.

Jack thought about a lot of things and made a call to Mark and asked him to bring all the men on the Core Team to the War Room in the next few minutes.

Jack looked up as Mark, David, Ethan, Charlie, and Elon walked into the War Room. After they sat down jack explained what had just transpired with the wives and the single women and him. "I want you guys to understand several things. First: I am on their side as I think the rest of you are. Second: This could be a big boost to morale for all of us and a unifying thing too. So, if you have any unhappiness about this décor project, let me know now or forever hold your peace. Because, I'm not crazy enough to defend you if you take a dark view of their, "upgrading" efforts."

Mark looked sternly at Jack. "I don't have a problem with the upgrading, but I don't think I'm happy about my wife and you hugging and kissing."

Jack knew Mark and Sarah better than any other couple on the Team. "Oh for goodness sakes, Mark. I just let them express themselves and made life easier for you." He grinned, "After all, the girl has to have some excitement in her life."

Mark was definitely in on the joke and he jumped up from his seat. "That is an insult sir, I demand your apology or it will be pies at ten feet on the poop deck tomorrow morning."

Jack leaned back and looked up. "I would apologize to you but, I think you'd like lemon meringue for breakfast tomorrow morning. You're on!"

Mark was about to confirm the challenge when Sarah came through the door to the War Room. "Sorry, but you two boys will have to vie for my affections later. We just got word from the Mossad that a team of military raiders about one hundred strong, stormed the Portal at the Sea Base and killed about thirty of the Mossad and a dozen Israeli citizens. They made it to the base level and were fighting against the Mossad and the IDF. They captured and tortured a Mossad agent and found out that we were not on their base but were on a big ship that was in the Harbor in Haifa today. The odds were mounting against the raiders so they retreated to the surface and fled from the portal in armored APCs. This happened twenty minutes ago. The Mossad figures that they have satellite coverage of the Haifa Shipping Harbor and most likely know that you've left the Harbor and are at sea."

Mark's silliness was gone. He looked at Jack. "Let's make sure they can find us." Mark spoke into the air. "Ethan, please make sure you record what happens after they find us. I also want you to hook the Mossad up so that they can see what happens." He used his battle/COMM. "All Troops, prepare for combat, Armor, FGs, and all weapons, MC out."

A strident alarm sounded throughout the "T" domain and the message was repeated.

Jack also used the battle/COMM. "R&D prepare the Formidable for battle and anything else you've got that is similar. I think we're going to repay the Albatross for the cowardly attack on the Mossad at the Sea Base." He got up and then told Ethan; connect me to the Director of the Mossad as soon as you can."

He turned to Mark. "We have to pray and make sure what we are doing is in the Will of God. Mark grabbed Sarah and the three of them praised the Most High and the Savior for guidance and understanding. They submitted their petition and waited, listening for God's voice. Raquel appeared suddenly. He turned his fiery eyes on Jack. "Go in the love and vengeance of the Most High." And he vanished. Jack stood up, "Gear up; we may have to make a statement on the ground."

Mark raised an eyebrow, "What ground? We're on a ship, remember?"

CHAPTER FORTY-FIVE

Jack was talking to Captain Conners when Ethan interrupted. "We must not have hidden our tracks well enough. There is a six ship fleet coming at their highest speed right up our six. WOW, with that speed they will reach us around, say, next week. Why don't you slow down so that we can play around 0200 hours instead?"

Jack agreed and told the Captain to reduce the speed on their vessel so that the other group can catch up around 0200.

The Captain laughed. "If the Force Generator is as good as it was in San Diego then I would suggest that we turn into them and meet them in less than two hours from now."

Jack remembered something he'd learned about the Formidable. He said, "Captain Maxwell, can you use the Rail Gun on the Formidable to take out several low orbit satellites?"

The Captain came back immediately. "No problem General. I'll get Colonel Reaper to map everything that will be in range when we meet the enemy. I'll take the Formidable out an hour before they are in range. Can you do the mapping for me?"

Ethan came back. "Ten-Four Captain, it will be ready whenever you want it. I've already mapped the birds that will be in visual range. There are two of them that are active and I can trace signals from both of them to an Albatross base in Italy. I will give you coordinates so that you are locked on by mathematics. Please remember that these two satellites aren't really enemy birds."

Mark frowned and looked at Jack. "What if they are simply overriding a military or civilian bird and we destroy it? There could be repercussions."

Jack smiled. "That will be their problems for letting a terrorist group use their equipment. Ethan said that he has triangulated the two satellites that will be in observation range when we meet the Albatross flotilla."

Mark smiled, "Yeah, but the military birds have flash recovery circuitry and will be back on line in less than five minutes."

Jack stared at Mark. "Not these satellites. I'm going to use the rail gun in the Formidable. I'll have Captain Maxwell climb up to the top of the Stratosphere where the air friction is minimal. There is approximately twenty-four miles from 70,000 feet to LEO or Low-Earth orbit. The EM or rail gun throws a projectile at a speed that will reach a satellite in less than two minutes and it will bring approximately 50 Mega joules of kinetic energy. That will mean the ten-pound projectile will be traveling at roughly 6000 MPH and will bring a force equivalent to fifty, three-ton vehicles traveling at one hundred miles per hour. It is sufficient to reduce the entire orbiting International Space Station to grain-sized particles in seconds."

Mark thought for a few seconds. "And if they fire a missile at the formidable the FG field will prevent any damage. Let's do it."

Jack looked at the remote vision port that reflected what was being shown on the control room of the Sword. There was only seventy-five minutes to collision time with the Albatross' ships.

Ten minutes later the Formidable lifted off of the deck of the Sword and quickly climbed out of missile range. Thirty minutes later Captain Maxwell reported he was on station and the warm up of the "gun" was complete.

Ten minutes till meeting time and the largest naval vehicle ranged the Sword with several 5" deck guns. Three minutes later the destroyer sized ship began to fire continually. The sighting system wasn't all bad. About one out of four hit the FG field and exploded. Mark's strategy was brutal. He told Captain Conners to accelerate to "ramming speed". The Sword quickly increased its speed across the water to fifty knots which would be around seventy-five miles per hour.

Captain Conners believed in the power of the Force Generator but old habits die hard. As he watched the big destroyer grow larger in the video screen his guts began to twist and tighten. He gritted his teeth and held the bow in a direct line to the amidships position of the destroyer. He was pretty sure it would turn to the right, because there was another ship to its left.

At the very high rate of speed he was traveling he was approaching so quickly the Captain on the destroyer had just decided not to play chicken and began an emergency turn to the right to avoid a collision. His waiting too long had the destroyer turning but not soon enough. He used the ship intercom. "All personnel brace for collision."

The Sword's Force Generator field struck the Destroyer two hundred feet back from the bow. The Sword tore through the ship like a sharp, hot knife traveling at supersonic speed through soft butter.

Complicating the understanding of the officers and seamen unfamiliar with the FG field, the field reacted like the one on the Formidable did in San Diego to the APCs it "nudged". That little bump blew the APCs a quarter mile away.

Nudging two APCs with a three-ton aircraft was infinitesimal to the kinetic energy the Force Generator field applied to the 8,900-tondestroyer when the indestructible front edge of the field of the 75,000-ton Marine Assault ship struck it at roughly 75 miles per hour.

In the blink of an eye the destroyer was shattered into hundreds of small and large fragments. Some of which were blown away from the Sword. Parts went up over two thousand feet. Some of parts were blasted down into the sea, leaving huge cavities in the water behind them. The bridge and the area under it, which were closest to the point of impact, simply disintegrated.

A five-hundred-ton section of the destroyer flew through the air and slammed into one of the smaller vessels, which caused it to explode and sink in minutes.

It took the Sword almost a half-mile to slow down and reverse course. The other three ships were running for their lives. Three missiles were launched from the Sword caused two of the smaller ships to explode and both sank in minutes.

The last ship was severely damaged when the missile destroyed its engine; which caused it to come to a halt on the surface of the sea. The craft was settling at the stern very quickly as the sea rushed into the massive hole and didn't have much time before it would slide under the waves.

Captain Conners was still shaken by the unbelievable damage the Sword had caused. He called Jack and asked if they should lend assistance to the surviving ship. It was navy tradition to help even enemy personnel in peril of death. Jack conferred with Mark and told the Captain to move over to the stricken ship. But, he warned. "Keep the FG on until we are sure they won't try to blow us up along with their ship."

As they approached the vessel it had settled by half the distance between the deck and the water since it had been hit by the missile. There was no one in sight on the deck or in the pilot house. Then, two men ran out on the deck and swung the deck gun around and fired it at the Sword with less than a hundred feet separating the two vessels. The shell hit the FG field and exploded. When the smoke cleared there was no damage to the larger ship. The two men stood there totally confused.

Suddenly, before anyone on the Sword could do anything, the smaller ship rolled to its starboard side and capsized. The smaller vessel went down at the stern and didn't linger. It continued to slide down into the water and with a large blast of air and bubbles it sank out of sight. The two men were pulled under the water by the suction of the sinking ship and were never seen again.

Captain Conners looked around and could see nothing but flotsam and debris on the sea. He estimated that the brief combat claimed the lives of over four hundred men. Mark ordered him to head North at fifteen knots.

The Sword moved away from where the short battle had happened and recovered the Formidable. Then they continued northward.

Mark talked to Captain Maxwell about the use of the Rail Gun. The smaller man grinned at Mark. "I fired two shots; one at each of the satellites, using the data Ethan gave me and scored two direct hits. There was nothing left, period. I watched the Sword as it struck the destroyer and vaporized it. These Kinetic Energy weapons are frightenly destructive."

Jack opened the battle/COM to all personnel and prayed for the peace of God and thanks for the victory over

the Albatross attackers. The men and women of the Sword
added their prayers as they were led by God.

CHAPTER FORTY-SIX

Ethan really liked the new version of the COMM/SEC department of the Crossfire Team. Now, of course, he was the only employee. The rest of the non-member team had opted to stay in Israel rather than continue with the Team for the next three years. But the new CRAY Ultramas were such a leap forward that Ethan and the latest version of Crayton were more than capable of handling things. Ethan had to admit that the majority of new tasks fell on the electronic back of Crayton but it all worked well.

Also, he didn't have a giant room in the middle of a mountain, nor did he have an equally giant room a mile under the surface of the Mediterranean Sea. Instead, he had a twenty by eighty-foot space in an Assault Ship called the "Kherev" in Hebrew or the "Sword" in English.

But, he could do thirty to fifty times as much as he could before thanks to the new computers.

He sat at his desk and reviewed the world events as summarized by the NSA and CIA in the U.S. and the Mossad in Israel. This had been completely refined by and scanned by Crayton but there were still eighty items that met the critical review criteria. Ethan took the top eight and summarized them for Laura and Jack. This day's events were starting out be a giant doozy. He sent the information to the War Room.

Jack and Laura stopped what they were doing and read the articles that Ethan sent them. When they finished reading the information they looked at each other. Laura looked grim, "Let's pray."

Before they could start to pray, the Angel Rose swirled into sight. She smiled at the two humans. "Hello and greetings from God on high. The Most High sent me to explain things about the battles to you. The battles you have seen in the news today are between two groups. The first group is made up of a violent population that has been out-populating the native groups that were beginning to lose their countries to the violent state religion. After the

Most High called the faithful to him, the balance swung more toward the violent religion. "

"Now, with Marco Marino limiting the freedoms of a good part of the world, the violent religious group has been defying the Anti-Christ and forcing new laws on the subjugated populations to extend their control. The two controlling factions are now facing off. The original populations feel disenfranchised and abandoned by the Anti-Christ and feel that the violent masses are attempting to subjugate them too, but differently."

"The original populations are now beginning to riot against both groups. This is bringing military law on one hand and violent revenge in the form of attacking mobs and riots on the other. As the violence continues to escalate millions of people will be killed and maimed."

"The Most High says that this is not your war. You may have to intervene on the behalf of believers but God will tell you when and who. You need to understand that this is one of God's curses on the people still on the Earth."

Mark looked confused, "I thought that the judgments didn't start until after the mid-point of Daniel's seven-year tribulation."

That is when many great judgments will occur. But, remember, this is part of the tribulations. The people of the nations that either didn't believe in God or didn't believe that God is a true judge. There are many people being judged at this time. The moon-god adherents believe that they can deny the true God and worship their stone idol that lets them do whatever pleases them. They are being judged throughout the tribulations. Some of the masses that did not praise and worship Yahshua are being judged by His Father at this time."

"After Satan takes over the body of the Anti-Christ at the mid-point of the seven years the seal judgments kill one-fourth of humanity as stated in Revelation 6:8. The trumpet judgments result in the death of one-third of those remaining as stated in Revelation 9:15. The bowl judgments do not result in massive deaths at all. Instead, they produce widespread intense suffering, and the fifth bowl which is the judgment of darkness, is focused upon the capital of the Antichrist as stated in Revelation 16: 1-16."

"These are things prophesied and are happening now and throughout the tribulations until the return to the Earth of Yahshua. That is why this is not your battle; nor your war."

Rose swirled into a blaze of white and gold and faded out of sight.

Laura shook her head, "Now I understand why we have to have faith and obedience all of the time."

Jack agreed with his wife. "Almost every nation has events of escalating raids and reverse revenge riots in all their major cities. The people who have been immigrating for the last twenty to thirty years have out-bred the original citizens and are demanding that they have the numbers to win any election and therefore they want to take over the customs and laws and make them like the ones where they came from. The citizens are tired of the demands and the violence that follows whenever the original citizens defy the wants of the incoming hordes and then get no help from Marco Marino's false peace one-world-government. The riots and revenge raids are rapidly escalating to all-out civil wars.

Jack thought about it for a while and then prayed for protection. He announced their next step and asked for five volunteers. He got fifty volunteers. He then selected the five he thought would deliver the message with the right attitude. He picked David, Alexis, Christi, Craig, and Kevin Steele.

He explained what he wanted done and how to deliver his message with the proper professionalism. They agreed and dressed properly and professionally and set off on their mission.

CHAPTER FORTY-SEVEN

Alexis stood back and evaluated Christi. Cute, blue-eyed, well-built blonde and dressed like a college girl.

Christi did the same for Alexis. Pretty, blue-eyed, well-built blonde and dressed like a college senior. Perfect for the mission they were on. The hard part had been making them look sexy while wearing body armor and carrying weapons.

David had dressed for the dad role while Craig and Kevin dressed to be young men of the age and physical correctness to match up with Alexis and Christi as probable husbands or dates. It had been easier to hide the body armor and the weapons. Most of the enemy would be men staring only at the women anyway.

The five of them had landed at night near Athens, Greece and took a cab into the town far enough before dawn to find a car rental agency and eat breakfast until the agency opened at 8:00 A.M. David rented a Chevrolet Tahoe with darkened windows to carry the five people downtown to the exhibition hall in the National Gardens.

They found a remote table that could seat ten to twelve people and settled down to wait. To the casual observer it looked like an extended family enjoying a vacation.

Craig looked at David and asked, "How long do you think it will be before our "company" arrives?"

David smiled, "Knowing Jack as well as I do, I'm sure he has communicated his invitation. I would guess that they will be here in the next half hour on the outside. Ten minutes would be more likely. Check your FGs for green LEDs. I'm sure it won't be too much longer."

Alexis smiled, "Good call, invitees at 10:00 o'clock.

Kevin kept his voice calm and steady. "Military back up at 12, 2, 4, 6 and 8 o'clock. Heavy weapons, RPGs, body armor and bad attitudes."

Craig smiled, "Show Time".

Four men, dressed identically in black suits, white shirts and patterned ties walked up to the table and took a spread position around the open part of the table. Sizing up the five people at the table, one of the men spoke to David. "I take it that you are representatives of General Malone of the Crossfire Team?"

David nodded his head and waved his right hand. "Gentlemen, my name is David and this is Craig, Alexis, Kevin and Christi. Please have a seat."

All four of the men had on dark sunglasses and the speaker reached up and took his off. "I find it very interesting, Mr. Zahavy, that you would use the correct first names for you, your wife and the three Steele family members." He smirked somewhat and casually took a seat. His three friends remained standing.

"I would have expected more expertise for a long time Mossad spy like you. Anyway, General Malone told us that we should meet and discuss terms for surrender."

The man's face hardened and he tapped on the table with each point he made.

"First, you will tell us how you destroyed our ships which had been sent to capture you. Then you will tell how you manage to avoid destruction when munitions explode around you. Thirdly, you will give me the names, ranks, and photos of each of your little terrorist team. They will all have to turn themselves in where I tell you, and surrender without fuss."

"We will treat you according to all NATO rules and ensure your protection from the people from many nations that want to destroy you all."

He deliberately ran his gaze over Alexis and Christi slowly and with a definite lustful leer. "I will personally interrogate the women. Of course that is to prevent any other person who might have inappropriate intentions."

David interrupted the man. "I'm sorry, you must be confused. This meeting is to discuss Albatross's surrender to us."

The man almost laughed. "How dare you te..." He stopped talking when he saw the smile on the two women's faces.

David also smiled, "Our message to you is; give up and surrender all of your armies, navies, air forces, and troops to a multinational military force for incarceration, trial, and judgment. Failure to comply, completely, with this demand will force us to destroy all of the things I just listed and we will accept your resistance as a defacto declaration of war between Albatross and the Crossfire Team."

The man sat there and laughed out loud. "Do you realize that we have the largest standing army, navy, and air forces in the world? We have over three million troops and more aircraft than the Russian and Chinese Nations possess."

David looked at the man soberly. "So? All that means is that it will take longer than normal. How do you answer?"

The man slammed his fist onto the table top. "I've had enough of this! I have over one hundred troops surrounding you and ten main battle tanks. You will not live to leave Greece. Every one of your Team will be hunted down around the world and I will dance on your graves."

David smiled, "Do you know how stupid you are?' David looked up and said, you aren't fighting us, you're fighting God."

As David finished talking there were multiple explosions outside the Exhibition Hall and thousands of explosive rounds slammed into the area around the hall. Most of the upper level windows were blown inward and many of them rained debris and the dead bodies of the Albatross' army fell to the floor. None of the five warriors flinched and watched the four men duck and cover. When the noise outside quieted down, the man crawled out from under the next table. He had a gun in his hand. His startled eyes looked at David.

David looked at the man. "Actually, you have zero troops and zero tanks around this hall. So, have you decided to accept our offer of surrender?"

The man's hatred showed in his eyes as he pointed his pistol at David and emptied the thirteen round magazine directly into David's chest.

The other three men died almost as soon as they started to fire at the five Crossfire Team warriors as slugs came through the broken windows.

David got up and went over and looked at the first man who stood there with an empty gun and fear on his face. David reached inside the man's jacket. David pulled out the micro camera and transmitter. Looking directly into the camera he said, "You have been warned, now when you attack us, we will extract a double portion from your group. You would be wise if you leave us alone. This is your last warning concerning us."

David tossed the camera onto the table and turned and walked out of the Exhibition Hall with the other four warriors. As they came out of the building, the Formidable landed two hundred feet away becoming visible as it touched down.

CHAPTER FORTY-EIGHT

After the Formidable returned to the Sword, the team debriefed with the rest of the Core Team. When it was complete and the After-Action reports had been filed, David asked Jack, "Did we deliver your message with the correct attitude?"

Jack nodded his head. "Yes you did, in fact all of you were perfect. Thank you for taking on a simple mission with such big results."

Christi looked at Jack, "I'm not sure I understand all the little nuances in that mission. Tell me what I am missing."

Jack smiled at her, "We wanted to send a message to the highest level of the Albatross group. That was why we set up a meeting and gave them plenty of time to set up a trap with overwhelming odds. I selected David because he represents a reasonable adult. He didn't look like a terrorist or a hot-headed insurrectionist that the OWG wants to have the public see us as. I selected the other four of you to represent the image of a decent family for the same reasons."

"I wanted to generate an image of reasonableness and honesty so that the public gets a better image of us. I did that for two reasons. The first was to show the world that God is still God and those that try to defy Him will lose. Just like the Albatross lost all their military assets. Ergo, the decent, rational family is protected by the Almighty."

"The second reason was to put the Albatross on notice that we will chew them up like puppy chow if they continue to act evil toward the Team. The Father told us to defend ourselves, but not attack them up the line until, just like the RHONE, the entire operation is to be eliminated."

"I give all the glory and the praise for this mission to Yahveh God and His Son, Yahshua. It was their idea. It was a natural next step after eliminating the ships that attacked us near Israel. It ingrains the notion that every time they attack us they lose. We needed a refresher course to back up the naval action. This was the smallest reminder but it came right on time to supplement the lesson."

The Core Team prayed, thanking God for the success of the mission and the strength to endure the next efforts by the Albatross to destroy them.

When Jack, Mark, David and their wives were alone in the War Room in the Sword, Sarah asked, "Why did they ever decide to name their group the Albatross?"

Mark chuckled, "Because in the earlier maritime services, the albatross was a metaphor for a burden to be carried as penance. At the time they did that, the Albatross was considered a bad omen for anyone who was subject to it. You know "A great weight" around a person's neck. The people who named their organization in the 1940s thought, incorrectly, that the name would be feared and people would go to great efforts to avoid causing the organization any trouble. We are planning to convince the movers and shakers of the group that being an Albatross will cause them to suffer it as a great weight around their necks."

The Crossfire Team will return in

"Global Crossfire".

If this story has awakened you or moved you to seek the love of Christ and His power for your life, whether you've never accepted Jesus as your savior or you've fallen away, repeat the following prayer and begin a most wonderful journey into eternal life with Him today.

Father God in heaven, As You said in Your Holy Word, (Romans 10:9) that if we confess the Lord Jesus as our God and believe in our hearts that by His Holy Spirit Yahveh God raised Jesus from the dead, we shall be saved.

(The prayer on the next page is a sample prayer when asking Jesus into your heart as your Savior. You can also pray this in your own words.)

Salvation Prayer

Dear God in heaven, I come to you in the name of Jesus. I confess to You that I am a sinner, and I am sorry for my sins and the life that I have lived; I need your forgiveness. I believe that your only begotten Son Jesus Christ shed His precious blood on the cross at Calvary and died for my sins, and I am now willing to turn from my sin.

Right now I confess Jesus as the Lord of my life and my soul. With all my heart, I truly believe that your Holy Spirit raised Jesus from the dead. Today I accept Jesus Christ as my personal Savior and according to Your Word, right now I am saved.

I thank you Jesus, for your unlimited grace which has saved me from my sins. I thank you Jesus that your grace that never leads to license, but rather it always leads to repentance. Therefore Lord Jesus, transform my life so that I may bring glory and honor to you alone and not to myself.

I thank you Lord Jesus, for dying for me at Calvary and giving me eternal life.

Amen.

If you just said this prayer and you meant it with all your heart, believe that you are now saved and have been born again.

You may ask, "Now that I am saved, what do I do next?" First of all you need to get into a spirit-filled, bible-based church that teaches the Scriptures, and you need to study God's Word.

Once you have found a church home, you will want to become water-baptized by immersion. By accepting Christ you are baptized in the spirit, but it is through water-baptism that you publically announce your obedience to the Lord Jesus. Water baptism is a symbol of your salvation from the dead. You were dead but now you live, for Jesus Christ has redeemed you for a price! The price was His atoning death on the cross. May God Bless You as you learn to walk in His light!

www.ingramcontent.com/pod-product-compliance
Lightning Source LLC
Chambersburg PA
CBHW060927180626
46817CB00004B/1422